Cowboys and East Indians

Stories

NINA MCCONIGLEY

FIVECHAPTERS
BOOKS

www.fivechapters.com
www.ninamcconigley.com

These stories were originally published in the following
publications:

"Cowboys and East Indians" in The Virginia Quarterly Review
"Pomp and Circumstances" in Slice Magazine
"White Wedding" in Memorious
"Reserve Champion" in Puerto del Sol
"Melting" in Forklift, Ohio
"Curating Your Life" in American Short Fiction
"Fenced Out" in The Asian American Literary Review

Book interior design by Maya Sariahmed

Manufactured in the United States of America
Published August 2013
First printing

To Nirmala and Patrick McConigley—
for staying through boom and bust

Contents

Ma despised Indians.

Laura Ingalls Wilder, *The Long Winter*
from the *Little House on the Prairie* series

Melting

We were the wrong kind of Indians living in Wyoming. There were Arapahoe, Shoshone, even some Crow. And then there was us.

We were the only brown faces in school and they called us niggers. The first time, I was ten. Before that, I'd just been invisible. I was playing tetherball during recess with my cousin Sunil. I was winning. A group of sixth-grade boys wandered by and said to us in loud voices, "Hey niggers, why don't you go back to the cotton fields?"

Sunil kept hitting the ball; it wrapped tight around the pole. I knew enough to be ashamed. Sunil was older than me, but had only been in the U.S. for four months; he was still slow with his English. Dried Sloppy Joe ringed his mouth, his breath made clouds in the cold air. I took his hand and we waited by the main doors for recess to end.

Home from school, I sat drinking my Tang and eating my samosa.

"What's the matter?" my mom said.

I burst into tears. Those boys were smart. In the spring they would be gone for calving; in the fall, hunting. They lived on ranches and would all have hardship licenses in two years.

Sunil sat quiet eating his samosa, his fingers slick with grease. *He was the wrong kind*, I thought. My mom asked him what had happened.

"Athai, some boys called us Snickers. I don't mind. Snickers taste good, no? It must be because we are dark." He continued to eat.

His affection for chocolate had grown in the four months he had lived with us. He liked that chocolate didn't melt here like it did in India. He was growing fat.

Cowboys and East Indians

I had been following the house for almost two miles and, while trying to pass it almost ten minutes back, saw its cross-sectioned insides laid open like a dollhouse. I half expected to see a family posed stiffly at a dining table, their legs straight out beneath the tabletop. But instead, a piece of cloudy plastic sheeting whipped out from the living room like a flag, waving me back behind the house at its crawling speed as it inched into the outskirts of Laramie.

It was then that I looked out the window and saw them in front of me, their black heads like notes marching up the scale of the shoulder. They walked two by two and one of them wore a long scarf that flapped like the plastic sheeting. I scanned ahead. The OVERSIZE LOAD sign on the back of the flatbed hung unevenly and the flash of the pilot car blinked into the dusk. I was going nowhere. I passed the quartet of girls and looked into my mirrors.

Yes. They were Indian. I pulled my minivan onto the shoulder. The house continued up Grand Avenue to where the road turned into interstate, headed perhaps for a foundation in Cheyenne.

I rolled down the passenger side window and called out to them as they passed.

"Do you need a ride? Where are you going? To Wal-Mart?"

They stopped and huddled like Christmas carolers outside the window. The thinnest one looked into my empty car and then stopped on my face. She smiled. "Are you Indian?" I didn't answer the question. I unbuckled my seatbelt and moved across the passenger seat to open the door. The thin one repeated her question, "Are you Indian?" I pulled the door open.

The girl tried again, "From India?"

I looked into their expectant faces. "Yes." And they began to climb in.

The thin one's name was Rani Mukherjee and she had been in the country ten days. The other three deferred to her. Their names were Suparna, Vidia, and inexplicably, Bunny, which I found very funny. Bunny was very fat and wore the scarf, which she wrapped around her neck like a mummy. Rani Mukherjee looked me up and down and declared I was from the South of India—she guessed from Kerala.

"Madras," I told her.

"It's Chennai now," she said.

I could tell that Rani Mukherjee was used to being right and being the leader of the pack. But I could also tell that Laramie had thrown her off a bit. I wondered if it was the wind or the altitude. She asked my parents' names and scrunched up her face when I told her Mike and Ellen Henderson.

"And my name's Faith," I added.

"Faith." She held it in her mouth like a wad of chew, then turned to the back seat and looked at the others.

I told them the short version. Left at a church. Adoption. Raised all my life in Torrington. No, I had never been back to India. I didn't know if I liked Indian food. I never knew my birth parents. I told them I was finishing my B.A. in Communications.

They had been walking to Wal-Mart to buy things for their new apartment. They were living together as graduate students in a small place off Third Street. They were all teaching assistants. But only Rani was going into the classroom that fall. The rest of them had flunked the incoming Summer ESL test at the University. Their grammar was beyond perfect, their knowledge of English far superior to that of any Chinese (who were common on the UW campus) or American graduate student, for that matter. But it was their stress and intonation that stuck them squarely in research positions. The speed with which they talked and the wrong stresses on syllables bought them a year of lab work rather than teaching. I wanted to tell them this was good. That I had had a teaching assistant for Computer Science who was Indian, and all of us had tuned him out. We laughed when he said simple words like hardware. *Hardvare,* he would say. And we would all roll with laughter. Another boy would do his own imitation of the teacher, stressing all his words like the Count on *Sesame Street*—all the V's emphasized like a DJ. It was better none of them was teaching. I could see Bunny would be eaten alive.

All of them except Bunny were in engineering. She was a mathematician. Which again, I found funny. We talked about their programs and they asked me if I remembered India. And what could I say? I lied.

There was for me a kind of memory of India. Of a place where I lived for two years before being adopted by Ellen and Mike Henderson of Torrington, Wyoming. Before I went to live with Mike the veterinarian and Ellen who worked at the sugar factory. My memory was like an encyclopedia of facts. I knew I was born in Madras (population 6.9 million), abandoned (on the doorstep of St. Joseph's, population 230), colicky (which affects 22.5 percent of newborns), not newborn (almost seven months, the May 1st birthdays of Saints James and Philip had been pronounced my birthday), and Hindu (there was a caste mark on my head when I was left there). And then there was the fiction of memory.

When people asked me if I remembered India, I would always say yes. *Yes, of course.* And I would lay out my memory like a list: I remember the sounds of the orphanage, the calls of the washerman outside, the smell of rice and sounds of bare feet slapping the cool tile floors, the Mother Superior's voice and the lullabies she sang. *Sometimes in my head, I hear Hindi*, I would say. Years later, I realized Hindi was not spoken in Madras. I must have heard Tamil. And so my story changed. But it all didn't matter much. My memories were not mine. They were my mother's; they were Ellen Henderson's memories. Ellen had told me about how they had chosen me. That there was a woman who brought a cart of groceries to the side door of the orphanage. Her cart was filled with long beans and mangos. She told me about the lullabies, the sound of the man who did laundry, how the whole place smelled like cooked rice. She also told me I was special.

And there were the pictures. I had studied them all. Ellen and Mike took only one roll in India. They were odd photos. Of children begging, people sleeping on the street, a cow with flowers around its neck, food and a cup of tea with a thin skin on its surface—pictures later shown on a screen as white as a block of ice, in our church basement as a slideshow. I had seen this slideshow over the years since I joined the Henderson house. When the church was raising money for some place, some place far away from Torrington, Ellen would bring out the slides like a roulette wheel and spin them onto the screen. If the church was lucky, the collection baskets would be brimming with cash.

And there were orphanage photos. Of its yellow and white façade. And there was Ellen, wearing a poorly draped pink sari over her skirt and white long-sleeved top, holding me. I was not Faith then, but Ranjani. *And there is Ranjani before she was Faith*, she would voice over as the slideshow moved to its dramatic climax. It's true I was skinny as a toddler and my shaved head gave me a grim look. In a tomato-red dress, my hair shorn, I look like a little black sheep who had met with an accident. My feet are in small orange plastic sandals. Mike holds one of my feet like a hoof. I would see him hold the feet of many animals over the years; it was his doctor's tic. He would hold the feet of dog and cow alike, looking at their paws or hooves as if they would give him a clue as to what ailed them, like they were some sort of koan. Mike is wearing glasses that were fashionable at the time, the frames big and round like pockets; he wears a suit even though it is hot and the air is thick. I would see that suit a handful of times before Mike and Ellen divorced twelve years later. Once when their other child, their real child, Cammie, made her first communion, once at a veterinary convention, and at an Elks dinner. Most Sundays for church he wore a dress shirt and slacks.

Ellen and Mike hold me like a prop in the courtyard of the orphanage. Mother Esther must have taken the picture. Mike and Ellen grin wildly. Their legs are cut off. Ranjani's—I mean my—face is blurred, but it looks to me like I am frowning.

There is only one more photo from that day. I sit crooked in the arms of Mother Esther and some other staff whose names Ellen didn't write on the back of the photo. None of them are smiling. All of them, except one, wear white saris. The odd one wears a smocked white dress and a white handkerchief on her head; she looks as if she is crying. I am like a spot of blood amongst the whiteness of their clothes. Their faces are the color of wet dirt. The kind of brown soil that collects in the grooves of horseshoes, packed until you pick them out. Later

I will think about that photo while working in the barn over some Christmas break.

The photos taken afterwards are clichés. Now I am Faith, asleep in new clothes on the plane. Here is Faith eating her first bit of Western food! Here is Faith with a woolen cap on her head and a new too-big coat! *It is cold where you are going,* they cooed to me on the plane. Here is Faith arriving with Ellen and Mike in Denver. The next photos are taken by Ellen's parents. Of me, Ellen, and Mike in the same pose as in the courtyard, but this time I am smiling. Cammie is there too. A little tadpole in Ellen's stomach. Cammie and I both were conceived in a country far away. Cammie and I both took our first moments of being in India.

We walked around the Wal-Mart. We looked at the pots and bathmats, and Bunny made conversions for them. When they converted from rupees to dollars, they walked away. Only Bunny bought anything, a disposable camera. She wanted to take pictures to show her family back in Pune. They all stopped at the jewelry case and made cracks at the quality of the gold jewelry.

"Nine carat!" This seemed to strike Vidia as inexplicably funny. I had a nine carat cross around my neck. It was a high school graduation gift from Mike. Vidia had a mouth of crooked teeth and a bob cut at an angle. Her hair was like origami, all lines. Her teeth were like crumpled paper. There was no symmetry at all.

I suggested the Dollar Store and when we arrived, I saw this was much more up their alley. Vidia and Suparna were practical, buying plastic trash cans, sponges, a fake plant. Bunny bought discount shampoo and a bucket. I was not sure what the bucket was for. Rani circled the aisles, taking it all in. And then slowly filled her cart. With two liter jugs of no-name pineapple and strawberry soda, clothespins, instant coffee, and also, a bucket. I asked them if they wanted to go to the Salvation Army. It was downtown, not too far from their apartment.

They were not as impressed with the thrift shop's wares and I could see why. The shelves were piled with odds and ends—decorative plates, figurines, old fishing reels, kitchen gadgets in immeasurable numbers. In the lined sections were sleeping bags with faded rainbows and army trucks on them, hand-tied quilts with patches frayed. Records, books, clothes—there were rows and rows of junk. It was all the debris of small town America. But then, they began to see the prices. Rani pulled out a thin silver phone and dialed. She spoke in quick tones to someone and then smiled at me.

"I told the boys they should come down here." She pointed to a chair marked $5. "There are many more Indian boys than girls at the university."

I knew this already. I had seen them playing cricket in Prexy's Pasture most nights before the snows came and turned the pasture into a slushy mess. Prexy's was a huge grassy area in the dead center of campus. It was first created for cowboys so they could tie their horses up there while they went to class. It was still in the university by-laws that they could. But I had never seen a horse there. Instead, in the late afternoon, one could hear the whack of bat against ball as a whole group of Indian men played cricket. When I walked by, none of them would make eye contact with me. I tried to smile, even stop and watch, but they all looked away. I looked Indian all right. I even had long black hair. But perhaps it was something in the way that I walked, in my lace-up cowboy boots, in my ranch girl jeans that said, *No, she is not.*

Rani came back to me holding a large pot like a baby. It was a pressure cooker and she was thrilled. It was $3.

"I can make curries in this," she said as she turned it over, inspecting its bottom, which was a little scarred with char marks. Suparna and Vidia also had their arms full—with wooden spoons, smaller pots, a full set of Corelle ware. Bunny stood by a microwave, her hand on top of it, staking it out as if she had summited its peak and wanted to mark the occasion.

The boys arrived, and more negotiations began. I was only brought into the conversation as I had my van, which could hold all the objects they were coveting.

"I can carry anything!" I said. And I meant it. I wanted them to have cozy places with pots and La-Z-Boys. Rani saw a mattress that was fairly clean and talked to a boy I would know later as Ash about whether buying a used mattress was, indeed, sanitary.

It took three trips in my van to carry all their loot home. In the end, they had a fairly complete kitchen. They also bought two chairs, one mattress, the microwave and a small TV with a grainy picture. Suparna purchased a painting of an abstract scene—all blacks and reds. But it was $5 and would give their home something more. She held the painting in her arms with an odd smile on her face, and I was not sure what she saw in it: the leering colors or the fact that she had been in the country not even two weeks and owned a painting. I thought, *She is the one I should know.*

My own mother Ellen also loves paintings. She would march down to the Goshen County Library once a month and check one out. They had a whole back room with racks of poorly framed posters and reproductions, waiting to hang in living rooms across the county. Ellen favored older artists. One month, Van Gogh's *Sunflowers* would be the centerpiece of the dining room, the next month Monet's *Water Lilies* would set the tone. She stayed away from abstracts and tried always for a motif of flowers and gardens. It was after Mike moved out and when I started calling them Ellen and Mike and not Mom and Dad, that she moved on to Western art. Russells in particular. Now we ate under the view of cattle drives and rodeo riders, prairie scenes with only a horse and rider blurring by.

"Haven't we seen enough animals?" I'd ask. Mike's practice was just down the road, and we lived outside of town, but not quite in the country. Occasionally when he had a particularly sick cow or horse, he'd tie it up in the corral we had in back.

Ellen would look at the scenes dreamily. "No," was all she would say.

When the last load was dropped off, I stood awkwardly in the door of their apartment. I hadn't taken off my shoes—they were boots—while carrying in the chairs. Now the girls stood in a row in front of me. It was Bunny who finally spoke.

"When we get settled, you must come and eat with us! We'll cook you all kinds of curries." She smiled warmly.

"Thank you!" they all chimed in unison.

I imagined us sitting around the table they did not yet have, eating out of the pots I had helped them find. Even though they were all dressed in jeans and T-shirts, I saw us all in white saris, just like the picture from India. I envisioned us sitting sharing food, laughing at white people. This last bit was a surprise to me. I had pretty much only known white people (except for Florence Little John, who was real Indian, native Indian). We had spent the years of grade school taking turns being Mary in various school Christmas pageants, since Mary was *Middle Eastern*. And even Florence, who was Arapahoe and also adopted, had already began to talk freely about whites as if they were nonentities. She ripped "Wyoming Native" stickers off bumpers and told me that if I was smart, once I finished school, I should go back to where I came from. That all of the U.S. would burn in the apocalypse. I told her for a native she sure wasn't embracing a philosophy of smudge sticks and spirits. She told me to fuck off. Poor Florence. But what could I say? I felt ready not to be in the minority, and standing in the crappy kitchen of the Third Street apartment I realized that, for the first time in my life, I was not.

I was called a week later to move two more mattresses. Another week passed, and I brought them a card table and chairs. And then, there was silence. At first I figured they were all settling into school. Maybe their landline hadn't yet been connected. But I remembered that silver phone of Rani's and knew they had a way to reach me. I had written my number on sheets of paper for all four of them. And my email. They just weren't calling.

Then, I got a late-night phone call from Suparna. She was over in the engineering lab, she thought she was sick—could I come? She might need to go to the hospital. I drove over. Suparna was waiting for me outside, even though the nights had begun their mountain cooldown. She now also had a scarf wrapped tight around her neck. I thought about the painting she had bought. The red splotches, the insistent black lines— enough to make anyone sick.

"It's my heart," she said, and then began to cry.

"How do you know?" I said. She looked perfectly healthy.

"Or it's something in this building. My heart goes bad when I am here." She motioned inside as if she was scared to go in.

"What do you feel like?" I picked up her hand and held it the way Mike held a foot. It was cool and dry.

"I am walking, and then, I get these shocks. Right through me." She stopped crying and dug into her pocket for a handkerchief. "I'll show you," she whispered.

We entered the building and walked along the hall. Outside the elevators that led to labs, she touched the metal door sides and swooned. I touched the same spot and felt a small shock, the familiar feeling of static. Of the combination of dry air and altitude. This was the same static Cammie and I delighted in when we were kids. We'd climb under the covers and shake our flannel nightgowns like flags. The green sparks and the crinkle of static kept us laughing until Ellen would come in and tell us to pipe down. That she had had a long day at the sugar plant, where she did the books.

"It's static, Suparna. It's not your heart, everyone feels it. It's just part of being in Wyoming." I had no better explanation. I was not the engineer. I was in communications.

Suparna touched the elevator door again and the same odd smile she made when looking at her painting came over her face. Her brown hands moved over the buttons pointing up and down. She turned to me and put her hand over my heart and held it there. She began to cry again.

"I miss home," she said.

"I do too," I said. My eyes filled with tears.

She took my hand and held it and we stayed that way for a long time.

The invitation for Diwali came forwarded by email from Rani. It was being held the first weekend in November, in the community center at Married Student Housing. Those apartments looked like low barracks, and I found them depressing. I could see that Ash was the organizer—his upbeat tone dominated the email:

COME TO DIWALI!

BRING A DISH! (ENOUGH TO SHARE WITH 10–12)

DRESS IN TRADITIONAL DRESS!

DINNER TO FOLLOW FESTIVITIES!

There was no address to RSVP to and someone had stuck poor clip art of crude flames around the text. I wasn't sure about the festivities or even what Diwali was, but I was happy to be invited. It was nearly Halloween and except for seeing

Vidia once in the bookstore, I had not run into any of them on campus in weeks.

That fall, there had been only one or two light powdery snows that melted, and feeling bold, I called out to Ash while he was playing cricket. He came over with a smile on his face. I didn't like him at all. He had a way of looking at me.

"I'm coming, I wanted to tell you I am coming to Diwali." I pronounced Diwali the way it was spelled.

"Di-va-li," he corrected. I thought about the computer science teacher I had. With his hardvare and softvare talk. His checked shirts and grey pants. His one black cardigan, which he wore throughout the fall.

"Right, Di-*va*-li," I repeated. I had spent nights learning the stories of the Ramayana off the Internet. I knew it was Hindu New Year. *I was Hindu once.* I even was trying to teach myself some of the prayers I found on religious sites. I had downloaded a recipe for tandoori chicken, bought the sauce from the Whole Earth Grainery on Ivinson.

"Have you seen the girls—Rani and Bunny? Suparna?" I asked.

"Yeah, we eat there most nights. We're like a family, you know, since our family is so far away." He eyed the action on the field and I could tell he was losing interest in me.

I had imagined them too busy to cook, heating ramen in their microwave. And now I knew they were having family meals. Was I not part of the family? *I was Indian once.* I thought of Suparna and me holding hands. I had tried to call her a couple of times and even left her a note in the engineering building, but she had not returned any of my messages.

"Come to Diwali. And you can bring anyone." Ash looked at me before he hurried back to the game. He turned back, "It's weird. You don't look Indian to me."

"Yeah, well, I'm from here," was my lame reply.

My boyfriend Cal had said the same thing to me almost two years earlier. He still lived in Torrington and we saw each other about once a month. I would go up, as I liked to check on my horse Bigger Bigger, who I feared was getting fat. Cammie and Ellen certainly didn't ride him, and Cal took him out about once a week, but Cal was busy on his dad's place. They farmed sugar beets and ran a small herd of cattle. My first two years of college I had been at the community college in Torrington and boarded Bigger with me at school. I wanted to live in a dorm and all the ranch kids were allowed to bring their horses with them. So after packing my bedding, books, and knickknacks, I packed Bigger into a trailer. Since I was a townie, I usually spent most holidays, Thanksgiving and Easter watching the horses of ranch kids. It was a great job. The campus was quiet, the stables with just me and the horses. It was cold all right, but I loved bringing hay and feed down to the barns and looking at all those brown coats and black eyes watching me knowingly.

Sometimes Cal would come with me and we'd inevitably end up making out against the stable doors, near where the hay was stored.

One Thanksgiving, post 9/11, I had been walking on campus when a group of boys whizzed by in a pickup. "Go back to your own country!" they yelled. I didn't have the time to think up a good comeback. I just stood there being mad. Because I was not Middle Eastern in any way. That day had been unseasonably warm—I was wearing shorts and a T-shirt. Did Muslim women dress like this? But I was mostly mad because of my *own country*? What did that mean, India? That wasn't my country anymore. Faith Henderson existed to prove that. Ranjani perhaps belonged in India. Faith did not. Faith barrel raced, played volleyball, and was a member of the FFA.

I told this to Cal as we finished making out that night. He was tall and skinny with a mess of brown hair that his mother cut in uneven strokes. The white skin on his face was almost always tan and freckled from being outside. "If I knew who told you that, I'd kick their asses." He asked me again to describe the truck. Did it have any bumper stickers on it? Did it have a hitch? All details that were lost to me, as I had immediately looked down at my feet and flip-flops. "I don't know" was all I could say.

Cal took my face in his hands and looked at me like he was about to tell me the most important thing ever. "You know, Faith, I don't even see you as Indian. I see you as Faith." His thumbs stroked my temples.

"What do you mean?" I asked.

"You know, I don't see you as brown."

Rani called to invite me to their house before the Diwali ceremony. I felt touched by this, until I realized they all needed a ride to the community center.

"How many can you fit in your car?" she asked.

"Six."

And then it was my turn to ask her for a favor. I had gone home to Torrington the weekend before and found the pink sari Ellen had worn at my adoption. I wanted to wear it.

"If I come early, can you help me get dressed?" I had no idea how to put on a sari but was taken by the idea of it. Of starting a new year in November, of wearing pink, of eating Tandoori chicken. Of trying out my knowledge of the *Ramayana*.

Rani insisted I come at 6 that evening, but when I arrived, no one was home. I sat on their stoop and waited. My chicken was in a covered casserole in the car, but the night was cold enough for it to keep.

Near 6:30, they all came giggling out of a house across

the street, and I realized the boys had moved in nearby. Rani wore a pink sari like Ellen's, but the bottom of it had birds embroidered in gold and the pink was deceptive: as she moved, shots of blue came through the silk. Bunny wore a long shirt and pants, with yet another scarf, and the front of her shirt was an armor of small mirrors. Vidia's sari was dark blue and very plain. Suparna wore a red sari with blue diamonds on it. It looked like a quilt that Ellen owned.

They looked at my blue Wal-Mart bag filled with Ellen's sari and a slip I had bought earlier that day. They ushered me inside and I was confused to see that the apartment was still quite empty. No pictures hung on the wall, not even Suparna's abstract. Besides the two chairs and the card table, there wasn't much else. Their mattresses were lined up on the floor. There were no dressers, and they all appeared to be living out of their suitcases.

"Where's your painting?" I said to Suparna.

"Rani made me take it down. She thought the red dot looked like a bindi and she didn't want the third eye watching us. I've moved it to my office." She adjusted the bangles on her wrist.

"Is everything okay over in the engineering building?" I asked.

Rani answered for her. "Of course it is. We're all doing fine. Now, let's dress you." She pulled out the sari and looked dismayed. It was rayon and quite cheap. Ellen had thought of using it for curtains in Cammie's and my room later, but never got around to it.

"Do you have a blouse? Or a slip?" she said.

I pulled out a pink tank top and the elastic-waist slip I had bought.

"Hmm, this won't work," she said, holding up the slip. "It's too loose." She eyed my jeans. "They'll work better—you need something tight at your waist."

They all took turns holding the tank top and each of them brought out an array of other blouses with more modest sleeves, each made by tailors in India. Except for Bunny's, none of their tops fit me. Years of barrel racing and riding had made my shoulders broad and muscled. Bunny's blouses poofed out in front of each breast.

In the end, I wore the tank top and jeans, and they all got me ready. I turned as they dressed me like a wound. They tucked the pleats of the cloth into my jeans and pinned the part that went over my shoulder to my tank top. Suparna got a brush and pulled my hair back in a tight bun. Vidia rolled up a tube of bright red lipstick and made a little dot between my eyebrows. Rani told me to take off my cross, which I did.

They stood back and took me in. They all looked to each other and began speaking in Indian. "What?" I said. I was tired and my hair felt tight.

Rani stopped talking and moved me in front of their bathroom mirror. My legs were cut off. But I saw myself.

"I'm Indian," I said out loud.

They all began to laugh.

The community center was only a short drive away, and yet I had to pull the sari up when driving. It felt like Christmas in the car, and Vidia brought a tape of Hindi film music to listen to. We laughed and giggled at the odd bursts of English that each song had. Rani held the pressure cooker she had bought that first day I met them. Suparna clutched a stack of bread that had cooked poorly due to the altitude. Bunny had a box of chocolates and Vidia two liters of pineapple soda.

When we arrived, it seemed like every Indian student at UW was there. And a few Indian professors and the Indian man who owned the University Inn. There were maybe twenty-four of us, but I had never in my memory been in a room with that many Indians. There were a few white people, some of them also dressed like Bunny in long shirts and pants. I would later find out one was an anthropology professor who had done her fieldwork in India; the other couple were Ash's host family.

A table was designated for the food and I put my chicken on it. I sat on a low couch and watched. The community center was actually very bare, just a big room with tables and a small kitchen. Ash and the others had put candles on all the tables. Confetti sprinkled the tabletops. Vidia told me in India they had sweets, lit clay oil lamps, and had sparklers. Sparklers were not allowed in Albany County.

I was ready for the ceremony to begin. I went over in my head the traditions of Hindu New Year, the Festival of Lights, how Ram and Sita's epic was finally over.

Ash went to the front of the room and began to talk. He was one of the only men dressed in traditional dress—also a long shirt and pants. Most of the other men were in dress pants and button-up shirts.

"Welcome everyone to Diwali! The Indian Student Association of the University of Wyoming welcomes you!" he began.

I hadn't known there was an association, and I wondered if I could belong. I thought about Florence Little John and how she told me to fuck off. *Fuck off*, I would say to anyone who asked.

Ash droned on about how welcoming UW was to them and then began to thank tonight's special guests. He asked his host parents, the anthropology professor, and me to stand. We clearly were *not* associated. The anthropology professor and I looked at each other. I think we were both embarrassed to be wearing Indian clothes. Looking down, I saw my sari was stained and realized that stain was made in India. I wondered what Ellen had spilled on it.

"And now! The special part of the evening! For our

entertainment, we are going to have a Quiz Bowl! Then we will eat all of the wonderful dishes prepared by the members of the ISA."

And so Ash began his questions. It was a *Jeopardy*-like game. He barked out questions about cricket scores, which movies Preity Zinta and Shahrukh Khan had been in, Indian politics—all things I had never heard of. I learned that Rani shared the name with a famous actress. Where were the questions on Ram and Sita, the meaning of the holiday? Bunny answered enthusiastically and in the end won a bar of chocolate. She squealed with delight.

When the meal was served, I waited last in line. I wanted to see how they all served it up, and I watched plate after plate fill with everything but my chicken.

"I followed an authentic recipe," I called up the line.

"You need a proper tandoor oven for it to be authentic," said Rani.

Suparna looked at the chicken and its rusty hue. "It's not that. I'm sure it's very good. It's just that, most of us eat veg—we are vegetarians."

All of us special guests ate the chicken. Ash's host parents told me it was real good. And then they asked me about beet production and how things were in our irrigated farming district. The old man had been a farrier and we talked about shoeing. He knew of Mike. The anthropologist was interested in how Torrington now had a sizeable Mexican population with the sugar plant. We sat at one table while everyone else moved from table to table.

Soon, round two of the Quiz Bowl began. Ash continued to bark out questions and I realized I didn't know any Indian film stars or how many test matches India had played against England. My car had been the only thing valuable about me that night. I walked outside and left the laughter and lit candles behind me. I began to walk to my car, but then continued towards the interstate. The sari was hard to walk in. I stopped and unwrapped it and carried the ball of cloth in my arms. The night after Cal told me he didn't see me as brown, he backpedaled. The next day, he told me I was exotic, and that was what he liked. I didn't know what was worse. *Exotic*.

Every year in Mike's practice exotic pets would come in. Pets who'd not adapted. Alligators, snakes, hedgehogs, sugar gliders, monkeys. All kinds of birds: lorikeets and macaws, cockatoos and galahs. Mike wasn't always so sure what to do with them, and he would make calls to bigger clinics asking for help. Sometimes I would help hold them while he inspected them, looked for the hurt. "People should not keep exotic pets in this place," he would say.

And then one holiday, while I was watching horses, I saw this llama in the barn. Ranches all over Wyoming have started using them. Some say they guard sheep better than dogs. The climate doesn't bother them, they are loners and need little care. One guy up in Lusk imports them from South America. It always made me laugh to pass a pasture and see a llama in the field. The sheep would usually be in a little circle, the llama out a bit away from them. The llama like a right angle propped up next to the geometry of ranching. And here was one in the barn. I walked over to the creature and began to change the water. It had a mean underbite and thin face. The next thing I knew, I was covered in warm vomit. Mike later told me it was spit. Instead of being angry, I respected it.

As I walked, I thought about that llama, who I later watched out in the corral while the Ag classes learned about that kind of sheep management. It was always away from the group, looking and watching. It watched the sheep with detached interest, but those sheep didn't dare move. *People stick to their own kind. And when they don't have kind? Then they are exotic.* I turned around and walked back toward the community center. The girls would need a ride home. I stopped outside. Rani laughed with Ash, Bunny ate her chocolate, Vidia and Suparna huddled with a group of older girl graduate students. I stood outside until I realized I only had a tank top on and it was freezing. But still I didn't move. The light shone out the windows. I gazed in at them and watched.

Pomp and Circumstances

The Shirley Basin seemed to be a big stretch of nothing that fell between Casper and Laramie. There was no cell phone coverage and not many houses except a few small ranches slipped between strips of cottonwood-lined creeks and the bases of rising hills. The basin at one time had been a forest. Lush, tropical, a swamp. Now every summer and into fall, people combed the sagebrush and scrub for petrified wood, for a small piece of Eden preserved. The basin is so rich with uranium that ghost towns once filled with miners lap at the edges. Low prices and oversupply has all but cut short business. In the early nineties, black-footed ferrets were released here. Once thought extinct, these little bandits thrive, feeding off prairie dogs and roaming the plains at night.

Rajah and Chitra Sen are heading across the basin to a graduation in Laramie. Their eight-year-old son Hari lies sleeping in the back seat. The graduation is for Rajah's co-worker's son, Luke Larson. Richard Larson is proud of his son, and has invited everyone in the office to attend the graduation. Rajah is the only one going. One, because he has never been to an American graduation and thinks it will be good for Hari, and two, because he finds Richard Larson hard to say no to.

For months, Richard Larson has insisted upon calling him "Senator." He has done this since he first saw Rajah's name on the thin wooden nameplate on his desk: RAJAH SEN. Now all the other engineers in the office, and even Bobbi the secretary, call Rajah Senator. It is a nickname that sticks, that perseveres like a fossil.

It is Chitra who states the obvious. "Senator? Didn't you tell them you are already a King?"

Rajah says nothing. He is the only Indian in the office. Hari is the only Indian in his school. Chitra is one of three Indians in their house. They are one of maybe six Indian families in Casper. She, perhaps, has it the easiest.

The drive is a little less than two and a half hours, and they have been silent for most of it. Rajah Sen thinks his wife is rude to the Larsons, as she had not wanted to come to the graduation. He thinks she is being difficult when it comes to making American friends. Rajah knows Chitra has been to the Larsons' house three times. One of those times, they went together. It was a holiday party. An event for which they were instructed to bring a "white elephant" gift. Chitra had selected a soapstone elephant from a shelf in their house. On its flanks there was an inlay of garnet-colored stones. But at the party, they realized they were not to bring elephants at all. They had gone home with a plastic reindeer. When you lifted its tail, small chocolates dropped out of its behind. Hari had screamed with pleasure.

Chitra has told Rajah that she had been invited for tea at the Larsons twice without him. With not just Richard Larson, but his wife Nancy. A thin, tanned woman who has a knack for matching outfits. She has deep set eyes and wears a great deal of eyeliner. Chitra also wears eyeliner. Kohl she has brought from Kolkata. Chitra's eyes look sleepy, the kohl making her exotic. Nancy just looks startled. Both times the Larsons had her over, Rajah was out of town. Richard Larson had planned that. They actually drank coffee and not tea. And the second time, Nancy Larson had baked. She had made a stack of lemon bars so thickly sprinkled with powdered sugar that Chitra looked as if talcum powder covered her sari.

Chitra has said little about the teas; except for she does not want to go back to their house again. If there is an office function, she would rather stay home. Rajah is sure that Chitra has done something to offend them. At the Christmas party, Chitra, who was not used to wine, told outlandish stories of India. She told Richard and Nancy Larson that hijras had danced at her and Rajah's wedding. That they were good luck. Rajah Sen saw Richard's face as she explained them to him. Rajah is sure that at the last tea something must have been said, as Richard too has not mentioned Chitra.

As they drive, Chitra thinks the snow fences look like abandoned snake skins in the grass. They curve and bend and then stop abruptly. These wooden skeletons hold more than the skin of winter snow. Along this stretch, some ranchers use the fences to create large drifts in the basins. It gives them a ready supply of water in the spring. It is still spring now, and the prairie is in a green-up. Magpies lunge along the roadside, the smell of sagebrush is sweet. Plodding red Hereford and black Angus populate patches of the plains. They are loose stock, as this is open range. Up in the hills, and on Elk Mountain, which rises before them, snow still sits on the peaks. A bit like Nancy Larson's lemon bars. Except underneath the peaks are rock and preserved things. Nancy's lemon bars, due to high-altitude baking and dry air, only stay good for a day.

When the Larsons first invited Chitra to tea, she was surprised to find Richard home. The invitation had come from Nancy alone. They live in a modest ranch house on the East side of Casper. Without all the holiday decorations, the house is spare. The living room contains a cloud-like couch, the tables all have ornate legs like curving columns. There are prints on the walls of Indian warriors wearing headdresses. There are the heads of deer watching them. Richard is a good hunter, and every fall fills their freezer with antelope, deer, and sometimes elk. Nancy brings Chitra a steaming cup of coffee. On the table is cream in a pitcher shaped like a cow. The cream comes out of its mouth. Their sugar bowl is from a different era. A small urn with hand-painted flowers rimming the bowl.

"Do you like Casper? Have you settled?" Nancy asked.

"Yes," said Chitra. And she meant it. Before they lived in Casper, they lived in Toronto for almost a year. Before that, they were in India. Toronto exhausted her. It was full of other Bengalis, and every weekend they went to Indian party after Indian party. Parties where satellite TV blared cricket or Indian movies. Parties where all the wives would put on their best saris and jewelry. Chitra would spend hours preparing chachchari or parathas. Parties where endless cups of tea were drunk. The talk would always be of India, or of the best schools to send their children. Here in Casper, they know few other Indians, and in many ways it is a relief. She can wear jeans and cotton tops, and when they are invited to any function, she simply goes to the bakery of the grocery store and buys donuts by the dozens, cookies with frosting the color of gods.

Richard Larson does not join them at first. He comes in after their coffee has been drunk, when Chitra is admiring Nancy's quilts, which she has spread across an overstuffed pink chair in the living room.

"So the Senator is in Riverton! Hope he's not gambling away your fortune!" Richard Larson laughs.

Chitra does not know of the casino there, but she laughs along.

Richard Larson takes a hard look at Chitra's sari. She had worn it because it felt polite. Because she was going visiting. It is a simple one. Blue rayon with a series of dancing birds on the border.

"I like your costume, your dress," he says. "I like the one you wore to the Christmas party." She is not sure if Richard Larson is flirting or stating a fact.

She had worn one of her wedding saris to the Christmas party. It was purple silk, ornate with heavy gold work. It had been stiffly packed for months, and so starched she felt she couldn't walk properly.

"Thank you."

There was a quiet at the table. It was just past lunchtime. A clock in the kitchen ticked a little beat.

"These fabrics are very pretty," Chitra said. She pointed to the calicos and patterns of the quilts.

"Yes, Nancy has an eye for color."

And then Richard Larson asks her for something she could never tell Rajah. He asks if he can try on a sari.

By the time they hit Medicine Bow, Hari is awake and asking to stop. They bypass the Virginian Hotel, which means nothing to them, and instead go to a small gas station. The inside smells of smoke. They buy sweet coffee and chocolate, then get on the road again.

Rajah takes in the wind turbines outside Medicine Bow. The town is almost bordered by them, and driving into the place, they look like cartwheeling crosses marking some sacred space. He thinks he is clever to think this, and begins to tell Chitra his observation, but instead tells Hari.

"Do you see those crosses?"

Hari scans out the window of their Honda and says blankly, "They are wind turbines." His class has been learning about green energy at school. Turbines are the newest point of contention in Wyoming. Some say coalbed methane brings salty water and that wind turbines ruin the view that so many flocking to Wyoming crave.

"They look like crosses, no?" There is a church near their home in Casper that has three large crosses like sentries posted outside their building. When they first drove by it, Chitra and Rajah had thought they were drying clothes on one of them, as purple cloth was draped on the arms like shawls.

Chitra squints out the window. She sees a pumping jack. "And that fellow then looks like he is bowing to Allah!" Prayers abound on the prairie for them.

They continue on their drive. The pumping jack pulls up more oil.

When Richard Larson asks if he can wear a sari, Nancy Larson leaves the room with a handful of quilts in her arms like a shield.

"You want to see a sari?" Chitra is not sure what to make of his request.

Richard Larson laughs nervously. "I'd like to try one on... if that's okay." He has lost the bluster she has seen in the office. He looks at his cowboy boots, which are ostrich and stippled like a pimply face.

"You mean Nancy wants to try one on?" Chitra is still confused, and wondering if this is a kind of trick. She wonders if this has something to do with Rajah at work.

Richard Larson is embarrassed. But then he gains back the same bravado she has heard when he calls their house looking for *the Senator*.

"It's like those people you talked about in India? At the Christmas party?"

Chitra thinks back to the holiday party. She remembers the white elephant, drinking glasses of wine the color of rose water. But she doesn't catch his drift. And then she remembers her talk about hijras, and how she found them happy, while Rajah found them a nuisance.

"Chitra, I am going to show you something." He pronounces her name Chee-tra.

She follows him into the basement, past a pool table and more deer watching them in a solemn line. He takes her into a room with wood-paneled walls. The floor is concrete. In the room are several large safes—or what Chitra thinks are safes.

"This is where I keep my guns," he says, pointing to a safe. "Kids. I told the Senator if he takes up hunting, he needs to get something like this. You don't want Harry there getting into guns." Nancy and Richard have one other child besides Luke. A girl named Gretchen Larson. She is in the army and stationed in Germany.

There is a narrow door with a lone padlock on it in the room. Richard Larson takes a ring of keys from his pocket and opens the lock. It is a small room, meant at one time as a kind of pantry. Inside is a little vanity with an oval mirror. A bench is tucked neatly in the middle. On the surface of the table is a wide array of makeup. Compacts, eye shadows that look like an artist's palette, brushes of all sizes, lipsticks lined up like bullets. There is a full-length mirror next to the vanity. It is also oval, and swivels on its wooden base. A stained-glass floor lamp stands in the other corner. Next to it is another plush chair. But unlike the cloud chairs from the living room, this one has a Victorian feel. It is an elegant chair. Light mauve with a kind of paisley pattern. It is not a Nancy Larson chair. There are framed paintings on the wall — and again they are different. They are of flowers, English cottages with thatched roofs.

But the thing in the room that delights her the most is a metal bookcase. Lined up are mannequin heads, all in a row. On each of the heads sits a blonde wig in various hairstyles: a straight bob, a curly bob, long Rapunzel-like hair, and a cut with layers framing the face. The mannequins line up and look like the deer heads they passed on the way into the room. Watching and taking it all in.

Chitra does not say anything, because she is genuinely unsure of what to say. This is a condition she felt a lot in Toronto. But since being in Wyoming, she has lost this to some degree. She appreciates not having anyone ask her why Hari was losing his Bengali, why she now cooked burgers, and didn't she know that Japanese cars were the way to go?

Richard Larson walks back into the room with the safes and turns the dial of one. Chitra half expects he is going to show her his guns as if they are similar to the display of makeup. But when Richard Larson opens the heavy door of the gun safe, it is like he has opened a closet. Inside is a rack of dresses. They are beautiful. They are the kind of dresses she has seen on TV. The kind of dresses as a little girl in India she thought American women wore. Her biggest disappointment since arriving in Wyoming is seeing how sloppy women are. In the grocery store she marvels and the loose sweatpants and stained winter coats most women wear. She has to give it to Nancy Larson — she is matchy, but dresses well.

There are dresses with sequins that look like silver fishes. There are taffeta dresses in which the fabric whorls in discreet patterns. There is a suit with Native American beadwork in the shape of flowers. There are slips like valentines hanging on padded hangers.

Richard Larson, who has for the most part been quiet, says this: "I am not gay and I love my wife."

Chitra nods.

"Nancy has known about this since before we got married. That's twenty-four years now. And she's okay with it. You have to know I am not gay. I just like to put these things on. It's not like your country. People don't consider it lucky."

Chitra touches a pink satin dress. It is strapless and has

a large bow on the waist. Along the hem is lace. She wants to explain the complexities of hijras, their place. But instead she strokes the dress.

"Okay," she answers.

Richard Larson sees her face. "Would you like to try it on?"

When they arrive at the graduation, they are late. They are unsure where to park, and end up walking in circles around the university campus. Chitra is wearing an orange sari and slip-on heels, so she struggles to keep up with Hari and Rajah who are both in sports coats, pressed pants, and ties.

"Do you want to go to school here?" she yells up to Hari.

Hari turns around and gives her a pained look. "Baba says I'll go to school in India. To IIT. Why would I go here?"

Chitra has no answer. She knows that school, Hari's schooling, should be her singular focus. That is why she has held off on having other children. Rajah wants more. She thinks of the IUD she had put in in Toronto. Her secret. Her own broken cartwheeling cross inside her uterus. It gave her a kind of power, a kind of energy.

When they find the stadium, they do not sit with the Larsons. Luke Larson is graduating in engineering. He will come back to Casper at the end of the summer and begin work at the same firm as Rajah and Richard. The Sens sit in hardback seats and hold a program embossed with the logo of the university. Inside is row upon row of names. Hari plays a pocket video game. If the ceremony is having an influence on his future academic career, it does not show. Chitra and Rajah watch as speeches are given, a woman sings, and as the graduates file out onto the stadium floor it is just like a movie.

As they walk out, the graduates walk two by two. In their black gowns and tasseled hats, they look like walking lamps. Their faces beam. They look fresh-faced and ready for the future. Chitra finds she is strangely happy and excited for these young people. For their accomplishments. For the future that lies before them. She follows their names in the program; she takes pictures of graduates she does not know.

Chitra decides that day in the basement not to try on the dress. Instead, Richard Larson takes her back into the little room and shows her albums of him in various outfits. When he wears dresses, he likes to be called Clara. Clara, from what Chitra can tell, is demure. Everything Richard Larson is not. She imagines that Nancy Larson has taken these photos, as most of them have been taken in the wood-paneled safe room. There are pictures of Clara in suits, in dresses, even in a velour track suit.

The only sari Chitra has is the one she is wearing. And so until she can next come over, she gives Richard Larson a taste of what wearing a sari is like. When they go back upstairs, she picks up one of Nancy Larson's quilts. It is a Log Cabin quilt, all in shades of blues and greens. It is thick and awkward. But Chitra drapes the quilt around him in a faux sari.

"It will look like this," she laughs. And Richard laughs with her, as the weight and bulk of a quilt are nothing like a sari. She feels amazingly light for knowing this about Richard Larson. The secret moves inside her.

Nancy Larson does not appear again on that visit. Richard Larson shows Chitra out, and she promises to bring back the purple sari for him to try on. Richard Larson does not ask her not to tell Rajah about this request, but she knows not to. It is unspoken between them. This kind of thing can get you killed in Wyoming.

The ceremony is long, and when it is over, they meet at Luke Larson's apartment. It is near the university. The apartment is filled with other Larsons and with Nancy's family, who are

Boyds. The Sens are one of the first to arrive and since they have never been to a graduation party, they all sit quietly in the corner until Richard and Nancy Larson arrive.

"Senator! Chee-tra! Harry!" Richard Larson exclaims their names when he arrives. He is wearing a kind of suit with the same cowboy boots he wears most days. Around his throat is a bolo tie with a turquoise stone. He has a large elk tooth ring on his finger. Nancy Larson is wearing a flowered dress. She smiles a thin smile at the Sens.

It is Rajah who speaks for them. "You must be proud of Luke! Such a lot of graduates! What a sight!" He is genuinely happy for Luke Larson and wishes his wife would also show more spirit.

"Yes, yes, you all get some food now," says Richard. He doesn't look at Chitra, which disappoints her. She has picked the orange sari because she knows Richard Larson will appreciate it. Western women just seem to notice a sari's color. But Richard Larson notices the intricacies of a sari. The weave, the fabric, the zari work. In fact, Richard Larson is the only person who has asked her anything beyond, "Are they hard to wear?"

When Chitra goes back to the Larsons', she brings a suitcase of saris. She has the purple one from the Christmas party, but she also packs a variety of saris. For fun, she puts in a salwaar kameez and a box of jewelry, which she has removed from the small safe they keep in a cupboard in their bedroom. It also holds their passports and visas.

Nancy Larson lets her in, and again, they have coffee alone. They eat lemon bars. Chitra finds herself driving the conversation. They do not mention the purpose of her visit.

"You must be missing Gretchen? So far away?" she asks.

"Yes. But we email." The clock's ticking punctuates her sentences. Nancy Larson is not a talker.

Richard appears as they are finishing their coffee. This time, Rajah is in Cheyenne, but will be back later that night.

"How do you like this weather?" he asks. It had been snowing on and off for a few days, and now the streets are a slushy mess. Chitra is still new at driving, and Richard Larson knows this.

"I have to get a big broom to clean the car. And wear boots!" Chitra lifts up her sari to reveal a new pair of brown leather boots. She had put on a sari especially for the visit, but had spent the week in sweats and jeans — she suddenly understood the women at the grocery store.

Chitra motions to the suitcase. "I have brought many choices." She walks over and opens the suitcase, and begins to spread the saris out on the same chair where Nancy showed her the quilts. She unfolds the saris to show the pallus, which are rich in decoration. She has a Kanchipuram silk sari, a handloom sari, a blocked printed sari — saris with fake crystals affixed in patterns like stars. She likes showing someone her clothes. In Toronto she worried her saris weren't fancy enough, but here, spread out across the upholstery, they look sumptuous, like wealth.

Richard Larson takes them all in. He runs his hands over the silks, the cottons, even the rayons. He is quiet. It is Nancy Larson who breaks the silence.

"I could make a nice quilt with these," she says.

The party is a tedious one. The first wave of family has been replaced by a second wave of Luke's friends. They are polite and well-dressed and dig into the food with glee. Nancy Larson has bought trays of cut-up vegetables and cheese from Wal-Mart. She has made plates of lemon bars and cookies. She has a slow-cooker filled with little sausages. Next to the cooker is a small crystal glass brimming with toothpicks.

Rajah and Chitra fill their plates with crackers and pieces

of carrot. No one from the party talks to them, except the occasional person en route to the buffet.

"What a pretty (costume) (dress) (outfit) (thing) you have on! And what a color! Is it hard to wear?" Chitra answers politely and for a moment longs for the Indian parties of Toronto.

Chitra is annoyed and cannot bear Rajah's stubbornness. She has told him that it was just tea with Nancy, that Richard came in hardly at all. That they didn't drink any alcohol (but she suspects Rajah thinks she did). But she knows that Richard Larson has become nervous. He cannot gauge her ability to keep a secret, and so stupidly has been silent and awkward at work. Poor Rajah! He cannot imagine what his wife might have said. He worries that he might never get a promotion.

The difficulty with Richard Larson wanting to wear a sari is that all of Chitra's choli blouses are too small for him. So instead she tells him to wear a T-shirt underneath the sari. But all of Richard Larson's T-shirts are walking advertisements — for races run, political candidates, for places they have traveled. And although his shirt advertising Sombrero Mike's in Cancun is a similar purple to her sari, it will not do. Chitra hands him the slip worn under a sari and tells Richard Larson to tie it tight.

"Tight, tight, almost like you can't breathe!" she instructs. And a few minutes later, he comes into the safe room in her cotton slip and a white undershirt. It is as if he is naked, and for the first time, he seems embarrassed.

Chitra cannot remember ever being told or shown how to wear a sari. Perhaps she watched her mother and grandmother so many times it imprinted into her very being. Richard Larson does not just want to wear a sari; he wants to learn how to put one on. And so Chitra shows him.

"First you make a knot like this, and tuck it in," she says while tucking the end of the silk into his waistband. It is the first time beyond a handshake that she has touched Richard Larson. Somehow feeling the soft give of his belly and seeing the paleness of his arms, she feels protective of him. She senses his vulnerability.

She turns him around and adjusts the pallu over his shoulder. She pleats the fabric. Richard Larson, as an engineer, is meticulous, and carefully folds the pleats into even amounts.

"It isn't heavy at all," he says.

"No, but walk carefully." Chitra takes out two large pins and discreetly pins the sari at the shoulder and at the pleats.

"Even I do this sometimes," she lies.

When she is done, she takes a long look at Richard Larson. It is as if he is no longer Richard Larson, but Clara. He stands very still, almost as if he is taking something in.

"I think I'll just go do my makeup," he says to Chitra, and she nods.

Richard Larson takes small steps to the little door, to his secret room, and then stops just as he crosses the doorway. He turns around and looks at Chitra.

"Do you think Rajah would think this looks nice?" It is the first time Chitra has heard him call her husband anything but the Senator.

"I think he would think you wear it very well," she says and means it.

It is when a series of toasts have begun that Chitra leans to Rajah. Hari, who has spent the entire party either eating cookies or playing his video game, sits quietly in a corner lost in his own world.

"They like me. I wasn't rude. Look, all is well!" she says.

Rajah says nothing, but pretends to laugh at the toasts.

"Stop this. I am telling you. It was just tea. Why can't

you understand?" Chitra feels shrill and wonders if the one glass of champagne she drank at the insistence of Mr. Boyd has gone to her head. She thinks she shouldn't drink, but it is hard not to with his co-workers.

"Fine," says Rajah. "Then promise you'll go again if they invite you — that you'll invite them over!" He seems like he is going to say more, but then Nancy Larson comes over to them and asks Rajah if he will take some group photos of the family. Rajah hates it that his wife doesn't have to work so hard to fit in, and takes it all so lightly.

When Richard Larson emerges from his little room, he has put on a full face of makeup and is wearing the long blonde wig. He doesn't look Indian — but he also does not look like himself. Chitra also thinks he is better looking than most hijras she has ever seen. When he is Richard Larson in his big boots, his aggressive nature is more like a hijra then. As Clara, he seems turned down in volume.

"You are looking very nice. Now just a few more things." Chitra digs through her suitcase and pulls out a flat box. Inside is part of her wedding set. Gold-dipped and not twenty-four carat. The earrings have thick posts and so they are out. But Chitra affixes a heavy gold chain around Clara's neck. Her bangles are all for her small wrists, so instead she wraps another necklace around his wrist.

"And now, for the perfect end," Chitra says. She lifts the folded paper in which a row of colored bindis are attached to a clear piece of plastic. She chooses a purple bindi with a small diamond in the middle.

"There," she says. "You are done."

Clara looks at herself in the mirror through the open door. And then begins to yell.

"Nancy! Nancy! Get down here, quick! Bring the camera!" he bellows up the basement stairs.

Rajah takes a series of photos of Luke Larson. Poor Luke poses with the Larsons, various relatives, and then his friends. Rajah directs Nancy, Richard, Luke, and Gretchen Larson in a series of poses. One is next to his graduation cake, another outside the apartment, by a late-flowering crabapple tree. Richard Larson jokes, "It's not every day you have a Senator taking your picture! Don't tax us for the photos!"

Rajah says little. And when the photo shoot is done, he hands Nancy Larson back her camera.

"Don't you want to see what you've taken?" she asks and hands the camera back to him. "Just press this to review the photos," she says, pointing to a small silver button.

And Rajah takes the camera.

When Nancy Larson appears downstairs, she is holding a camera. She walks past Chitra and goes straight for Clara. She takes his hand and strokes his hair, she fingers the bindi on his forehead, and she runs her hand over the purple silk. She then turns to Chitra.

"Thank you. He looks, I mean Clara, looks beautiful."

Chitra feels like she is once again in a world she doesn't know. And while Nancy Larson begins to take pictures, to talk to Clara in a low voice, Chitra excuses herself to the bathroom.

When she comes back, she sees that Nancy is looking through her saris. She is holding a simple handloom that is also purple.

"Would you like to try it on?" Chitra rummages around for a choli and slip.

Nancy Larson looks like she is going to say no, but she looks at Clara, who now is sitting in her chair in the little room. She looks again to the sari.

"Yes," she says. "I would like that very much."

Once Nancy Larson is in her sari, it is Chitra who takes

photos of the two of them against the pine wall. She instructs them to fold their hands in Namaste, which they do. They pose with their arms around each other, and Chitra is glad she has pinned them both into their saris.

It is when the photo session is over that Clara/Richard Larson turns to his gun safe and spins open the combination. He pulls out the pink dress that Chitra had held on her last visit.

"You have to try this on," he says. Without pausing, Chitra takes the hanger with the pink satin dress, she takes a short blonde wig. She heads into the little room. The temptation is too great. And when she comes out, she feels like she is part of something for the first time. She poses with Clara, and then with Nancy, and then they use the timer to take a shot of them all. They all laugh as the Larsons' saris fall off the shoulder, as they pool to the ground like a swirl of cream.

When Rajah Sen begins to review the photos of the graduation, he continues to go back, back, back. He examines a series of pictures of Nancy Larson's latest quilt in progress. It is the Ohio Star pattern and the fabrics she has picked are very nice indeed.

Once all the saris are packed up, Chitra keeps out two saris. They are cheap ones. One is rayon and the other a kind of fabric that looks like, but is not, silk.

"For you," she says and hands them to Nancy and Richard Larson. Nancy Larson in turn gives her a plate of lemon bars. She hands Richard Larson a packet of bindis. He has tried to give her the pink dress, but she doesn't want it. It would be hard to explain, and she cannot imagine wearing such a dress out in public. The very immodesty of it surprised her when she put it on. She doesn't need it to feel American.

They will not ask her to come again, and she imagines they will not talk of this. That in several months there will be another white elephant party where the only elephant in the room will be this day. Chitra will know to buy a joke, a laugh at someone else's expense. She will tell another story of India, this one with a tiger, or how at her wedding they had six-hundred guests, which was considered not a big wedding at all.

As she leaves the Larsons' house, she is almost blown over by the wind. Their house is sparsely landscaped with no mature trees. She feels the wind deep in her bones.

Chitra sees Rajah with the camera in hand, and comes over and puts her hand on his. He has gone back, but not far enough.

"Did you take good pictures?" she asks and takes the camera. Rajah has been studying the star quilt with intensity.

"Okay," says Rajah. He repeats what Nancy Larson said months ago. "Your saris would make a nice quilt."

"Are you an idiot? I would never cut them!" Chitra laughs. "But I'd cut your mother's." Chitra's mother-in-law has given her a series of bland old lady saris.

Rajah laughs, as he hates his mother's taste. Chitra pulls a wrapped Waterman pen set from her bag.

"I bought Luke some pens. Engraved."

And Rajah is touched by his wife's thoughtfulness. Although the day has not enchanted Hari, he is happy to see that seemingly all is fine between the Larsons and Chitra. That the day has gone on without a hitch.

The Sens say goodbye to the Larsons and begin the trip home. She is once again given a plate of lemon bars for the road.

They drive. They are near Como Bluff, and Hari has spent the last half-hour talking of dinosaurs. It is not the graduation that has caught his attention, it is the idea that just beyond the hills is a graveyard of bones. He tells them theories of extinction, facts about the size and speed of these creatures that roamed the earth before humans ever existed. He tells them that there are wagon ruts from the Oregon Trail not far away. That pioneers crossed this way.

They stop again at the same convenience store in Medicine Bow and they take turns using the bathroom. When Chitra comes out, the clerk eyes her with suspicion. Hari is already outside, combing the parking lot gravel for fossil finds.

"You have to buy something to use the bathroom," the clerk says.

Rajah scans the shelves of beef jerky and cigarettes, soda and hot dogs.

"We're not hungry," he says pleasantly. "My son, he needed to use the toilet."

The clerk sighs, "You have to buy something."

Chitra thinks Rajah is going to bend, to buy a pack of gum or a postcard. He pauses at a postcard of a prairie dog proclaiming that *Someone in Wyoming Loves You!*

It is Chitra who moves in front of him. "Don't you know," she says to the clerk. "He is a Senator. A King. He can do whatever he wants, whatever he pleases."

"I didn't know that," says the clerk and snorts. And then she goes back to arranging matchbooks in a small display on the counter.

Chitra takes hold of Rajah's hand. Her skin is dry, and his hand is warm. He opens the door and they walk two-by-two into the sun, into the wind.

Split Estate

It was the second day that Worm had brought his son Will out to the rig. The first day the child had stayed in his truck, his blond head occasionally bobbing above the seats. Lewis observed the child letting himself out for a breath of fresh air, a slight stretch. He watched the boy pee on the wheels of the cab and hoped the toolpusher, who only visited the rig for an hour or so a day, would not see the child. Years ago, no one cared who wandered on and off the site. But with insurance being the way it was, anyone not authorized was frowned upon.

On the first day, Lewis limped up to Worm.

"Your kid, he isn't allowed here," he said.

"Shit, man, I know. What am I supposed to do? Will's mother's gone to Vegas. She's gettin' married in the Star Trek Lounge. She just dropped him off. What am I supposed to do?" Worm laced his gloved fingers. His ex-girlfriend and the mother of the boy lived in Jeffrey City and was "a real piece of work." Worm had never mentioned the boy before showing up with him that morning.

"It's the insurance. You could get fired. Don't you know

anybody?" Lewis hated this shit. Roughnecks. You could always count on them to be stupid.

"You know as good as I do. We all stay in the same motel. I don't know anyone in Gillette." He shifted his weight from foot to foot. "I asked one of the maids. Told her I'd pay her. But shit, she's got rooms to clean." Worm looked to the truck. His son's head was bent over a video game. "He won't make trouble. He's a good kid."

Lewis let it go. It wasn't his problem.

On the second day, it was Worm who approached Lewis. The spring had brought heavy snows, and a green-up was predicted. The rig had been shut down several times due to temperatures, mud, and the Bureau of Land Management. The weather had fluctuated between warm spring days with high sun to snowstorms in which the snow blew in wide wet flakes like paper. That morning it had snowed for hours, and the muddy makeshift road across the Cane Ranch was covered. As Lewis had eaten his breakfast in the lobby of the Castle Court Motel that morning, he had heard the snow was to taper by late afternoon. A Chinook was thought to be coming.

"What's wrong? Why you limpin'?" Worm asked, sidling up to where Lewis was working.

"Gout." Lewis's gout was neither rich man's nor poor man's, as Lewis was firmly middle class and had made a life of avoiding any extreme. He didn't drink and except for a fondness for a good ribeye, his gout remained a mystery, his deformed foot a monstrosity.

"Gout?" Worm asked.

"It's like arthritis. It's hard for me to put on my fucking boot." Lewis pointed down to his muddy steel-toed work boots. "I just got to drink water. And eat cherries. Cherries are good for gout. But they aren't in season." He had gone to the Wal-Mart the night before asking for cherries. A girl with a black eye and a ring on every finger led him to the baking aisle. She handed him a can of pie cherries in which the fruit was clotted together by sugar and gelatin.

"That's tough. Real tough goin'. Especially with the weather." Worm paused. "Hey, you think my boy Will can sit in the unit? It's awful cold today." He motioned to the gas detector unit, the only shelter on the site.

"Shit, Worm. I could get in real trouble here." Lewis looked to Worm's truck. The engine idled. Snow covered the windows. But the sky was already beginning to lighten.

"Today's the last day. I called my parents up in Lovell. They're gonna watch him. I'm gonna drive him tonight. When the rig shuts down." A peak of snow covered the top of Worm's red hardhat.

"Tell him not to touch anything," Lewis said. "That equipment is expensive."

Worm was already walking to the truck, ignoring Lewis's last words.

For Lewis, who was the geologist, the trailer unit was his office. When there was no trailer, he worked from his truck. Coalbed methane wells were a much tidier affair than oil rigs, which ran twenty-four hours a day. Methane wells ran from 8 a.m. to 5 p.m., and all the workers, from the derrick man to the engineer, could be filling their plates at the Golden Corral in Gillette by 6 p.m. Coalbed methane wells worked well for Lewis. After years of being called away when drilling had sped up or stopped, after missing Christmases and birthday parties due to the unpredictability of oil, he had found salvation in gas. Gas, which except for the water tables that sometimes flooded the Wyoming prairie, worked like clockwork. In the old days, when Lewis would stay out on the rig, there were a few trailers and they slept in shifts. When Lewis went to sleep at night, he could smell the driller, who slept before him, on the sheets. A musky smell of chew and coffee. When he would arrive back home in Casper, his wife Petra would hug him and then scrunch her nose.

"Go take a shower. You boys on the rig stink." She'd look to their son Donald who hid behind her legs. Donald always took a few hours to warm up to Lewis when he came back home. "Don't your daddy look a bum? Maybe this isn't your daddy." Lewis's clothes were stained with sediment and grease. His hair was flat from his hardhat and baseball cap. A beard would often outline his face.

"I'm your daddy." He would say. *"I'm your daddy."* He would repeat it as if to convince himself that he was home and the rig was another place, far away.

Nowadays, the crew all stayed in town. Except for their trucks, there was little on the site besides the well. The gas detecting unit wasn't there all the time. But the trailer was set up now, and there was a little bunk and table. The rest of the trailer was filled with equipment.

He called out behind Worm, "We're going to Deadwood tonight. The rig's shutting down early. You could be in Lovell just past dinner. We're going to Deadwood tonight!"

"Yeah. We all know you're going to Deadwood," he replied.

Worm was already at the truck, opening the door for Will to jump out. The boy was around seven or eight. Lewis squinted at the child. He was tall all right. And skinny as the trunk of a lodgepole pine. The boy was wearing sweatpants and a T-shirt without a coat. He stumbled out of the cab holding a bulging blue Wal-Mart bag in his hand. He trailed behind Worm.

Billy Hatton, the other roughneck, called down from the mast of the derrick. "Woo-hee, they're getting 'um earlier and earlier. You gonna be a roughneck like your daddy?"

"No." Will's voice was loud and ringing. His skin was sallow and slightly blue, his face vulpine.

"He's gonna do bareback in the rodeo. You should see this kid ride a horse." Worm turned around and pushed Will in front of him. "Do you remember that time you rode a horse? Up there in Lovell, near Grandpa and Nana? You can ride a horse again. Soon. Maybe tomorrow." Will and Worm stopped in front of Lewis.

Up close, Will had the same ears as Donald, ears that stuck out like handles on a sugar bowl. When Donald was little, Lewis would pretend to twist his ears like dials on a radio. Will's eyes had the same watery expression. Will smiled and Lewis turned away from him.

Lewis limped to the trailer. Every time his joints bent, he cringed. That morning he had gazed at his throbbing foot. Uric acid gathered in a fat mound on the side of his big toe. It was as if he had grown another one. The area was red and shiny. He opened the door and moved to the small heater.

"Keep that bag there away from this. Don't touch anything. It's all very expensive. Do you have stuff to do?" Lewis asked.

The boy nodded.

"He's got one of them video games. He's fine. I bought him some magazines at the Wal-Mart. And he's got a puzzle. Don'tcha have a puzzle there, Will?" Worm said.

Will nodded. Lewis pulled out a stack of paper gas charts from his briefcase. The lines on the paper looked like a chart recording a heartbeat. He handed the log to the kid.

"You can draw on this. On the back. Or pretend you're a doctor." He looked at Worm. "You better get him out of here by 3. The rig's shutting down. We're all going to Deadwood." He shut the door behind him.

The trip to Deadwood was a reward for reaching a certain level of production. Bow Energy was now producing 25 million cubic feet of gas a day. It was a milestone, as bad snow, environmentalists, and irate ranchers not wanting roads to be put across their land had caused a winter of stagnation. For a short time, the rig closed so sage grouse could mate. The males drummed up and down the prairie, parading their yolk-yellow chests through their feathers. On other rigs Lewis had worked, they closed down for burrowing owls. Ned Cane, who owned the ranch they were working on, had only allowed Bow to come in after months of arbitration. He would ride his horse or sometimes his ATV near the well-pad and just stare at them. Sometimes he would holler at them. Telling them his family had homesteaded the land, and they were thieves.

Deadwood was a two-hour-plus trip from Gillette — almost an hour to the South Dakota state line — and the rig was to shut down early, allowing them to get to Deadwood in time for a prime-rib dinner and a little gambling.

The drillers, who did not work for the energy company, but for a drilling contractor, were not invited. It was a Bow Company party. The complaints of this injustice had been voiced for nearly two weeks. Worm and Billy had tried to convince the company and then Lewis they should go too. Even their boss, a driller named Staines, echoed their whine.

"Shit, Lew, you don't work for Bow. Why do you get to go?" Billy had said at dinner at the Golden Corral two nights ago. His mouth was full of salad laden with ranch dressing. He had a tattoo of three tears going down his face.

"'Cause he's the geologist." Worm said. "He knows if they're gonna be rich. If he ain't around, who's gonna know what's down below?"

Lewis shrugged. He was a consulting geologist. He worked for Bow all right. They signed his checks. They also didn't give him health insurance, benefits, or any vacation. Bow was as good as any company he had worked for, and in the past years he had worked almost exclusively for them. Now that Lewis was five years shy of retirement, he thought maybe he had gotten it all wrong. His consulting had left him with no reward for loyalty. They would depend on Petra's retirement, her money from years of working for the city. Donald wasn't going to watch over them in the golden years. He was addicted to meth and came home every few months, his own clothes stained and a beard across his face. *Are you my son? Am I your daddy?* Lewis's head would whirl when he saw him.

"I bet you see some Indians up there in South Dakota. That movie, the one with the dancing wolves — that was filmed near there. I sure would like to see some Indians. My granddaddy was part Cherokee." Billy looked at Lewis as he spoke.

"Shut up," Worm said. "You could go down to Lander if you wanted to see some Indians. And you ain't part Indian. Though you got a regular trail of tears there on your face." Worm laughed and put his spoon deep into a tower of soft-serve.

At 3 p.m. the drill pipe stopped turning. The child had stayed in the trailer and ignored Lewis when he came in and out of the unit. At lunchtime, Worm had gone to the truck to get a paper bag with a greasy corn dog in it for the kid. Worm himself ate very little but drank mugs of soda. He had a gallon mug as big as a vase that he kept filled with Mountain Dew. Lewis wondered if he was on meth.

The child opened the door only once during the day. The door had flown open after lunch and Lewis registered the look of surprise on the child's face. His mouth made a perfect O as his hands moved to his ears. The clank of pipe and the rotary table rotating startled him. He scanned for his father, then scrambled to shut the door. Lewis went back to his work. It had stopped snowing and Lewis laid samples on the ground. Shale, sandstone, and coal sat upon the snow. The shales came in all colors and looked like jewels upon the whiteness. It was enough of a jackpot for Lewis.

For the trip, Bow Energy had hired a bus from the city. Originally, it was to pick up Lewis from the rig. The toolpusher said he might as well be picked up there as well. But Ned Cane had raised a fuss about a bus coming into his place and then the snow had covered the makeshift roads anyway. Now Lewis was to meet the bus in Gillette, in the parking lot of the Castle Court. All of Bow's employees from the Gillette office — from the company man to the secretary — were going on the trip. Even folks from the head office in Denver were coming. Most people were bringing spouses, who were also invited. The toolpusher's wife had once won $50 in the Colorado lottery. The toolpusher told Lewis his wife was always lucky, except when it came to marrying him. Lewis had asked Petra if she wanted to join in on the trip.

"Who goes on a trip on a Thursday? You know I got to work on Friday. I can't leave home." Petra frowned at the imposition of being asked. Lewis knew she didn't want to leave the house. In case Donald came home. Two months ago they had gone to Denver for a hockey game. When they came home, the house had been robbed. TVs, their stereo, furniture, his rock collection, and Petra's jewelry were all gone.

As Lewis prepared to leave the rig, the silhouette of Ned Cane was visible in the distance. He walked over to Billy and Worm.

"You get that kid and go. If Ned Cane sees him, you can bet we'll have people out here tomorrow raising hell." Lewis motioned to the trailer.

"We're outta here. Goin' to Lovell. To my folks." Worm headed for the trailer.

Billy ignored Worm. "Look for Indians, Lew. Maybe you'll get lucky."

Worm stopped and turned back around. "Indians are good luck. Seeing one will bring you nothing but luck," he said.

"Make sure you get that kid out of here. I got to go back into town," Lewis said, heading for his truck.

Lewis thought about Indians and their luck on the drive back to Gillette. When he first came to work on Ned Cane's ranch, Ned had invited him to coffee. Unlike most ranchers, who leased their land from the government, Ned's family had homesteaded the ranch. It was his. In the bust in the 80s, Ned became desperate for money. His scraggly bunch of Red Angus wasn't making him two pennies to rub together. In a moment of desperation, he sold the mineral rights and didn't even keep a small royalty. If he had, he would've been a millionaire today. Now it was a split estate, he only had the surface rights. Ned had lamented this fact to Lewis. Knowing that Lewis was the geologist, he whined about how this land was his, how the oil companies had screwed him. He connected with the Outdoor Wyoming Council and had hopes that the greenies would stop the drilling. Lewis looked around while Ned talked. His small cabin was filled with crap. Magazines, old furniture, a case of arrowheads. Ned noticed his gaze.

"I found all of them out there. Walking around. Tepee rings too. All sorts of things," Ned beamed.

"Looks like those Indians lost more than their mineral rights," Lewis joked. Ned hadn't laughed.

When Lewis pulled up into the Castle Court, the bus was already waiting. Lewis parked and boarded the bus. He struggled to walk without a limp. Climbing the short flight of stairs, he took in his breath quickly. His legs felt as if they would buckle. He had wanted to call Petra before he left, to tell her he was on his way. But instead he took a seat alone behind the toolpusher and his wife.

"Trail mix?" The toolpusher's wife handed him a bag from her lap.

"No." When Lewis's gout was in full swing, he watched his diet and tried to stick to greens and water.

The bus took I-90 to Spearfish, where they veered off onto a smaller highway to Deadwood. The roads had been sanded and the mix of snow and sand made a kind of slurry on the road. Lewis hoped that Worm drove to Lovell slowly. Out the window, the clouds made shadowed birthmarks on the prairie. Drifts piled up against the snow fences. The group craned to see Devil's Tower out the window. In the dusk, they could make out its cylindrical shape. They stopped near Sundance for snacks. The toolpusher's wife bought powered sugar donuts and sweet coffee.

When they arrived in Deadwood, it was near 6 p.m. The bus parked outside the Golden Strike Casino. The vice president of Bow, who weighed near three-hundred pounds, made a speech about production levels and why energy was so important, especially here in the U.S. of A. As each person left the bus, he handed the employees a book of drink coupons and ten dollars worth of chips. He wished them luck.

Lewis staggered off the bus. He could hardly walk.

"You okay there?" asked the VP.

"Just stiff." Lewis tried to smile. "I'm not used to sitting around. You boys keep me on my feet on the rig."

"Win big. Then you can retire early," the VP joked.

Since it was a Thursday, half of the casino was closed. Metal gates closed off rows of slots, several blackjack tables were empty. There was a feeling of low expectations. When Lewis had once asked Petra if she was disappointed that they didn't have more kids, that Donald turned out on drugs, she shrugged. "I was raised on a ranch. I learned to keep my expectations low."

Yet the half that was open was buzzing. Twilight-colored lights flickered and winked at the party. The VP moved ahead of Lewis and led the way to the dining room, which was named *Midas's Table*. Lewis took a seat near the end of the big table that was set for them. Plates of steaming prime rib, mashed potatoes, and salad were placed in front of each employee. Lewis picked at the food. Eating the prime rib would only make the gout worse. He cut the meat into tiny bits and tucked it underneath the potatoes. The toolpusher ripped a coupon out of his book and handed it to a tuxedo-clad waitress.

"Get my friend here a drink. What you drinkin', Lew? Beer? Whiskey?" His face flushed red from the food and excitement.

"I think I'll take it easy." Lew smiled. "Maybe just some coffee. I bet they got some good coffee here. I'm getting too used to that shit at the Castle Court."

"He'll have a Seven and Seven." The toolpusher ate a bite of his food.

When the drink came, Lewis took small sips. How he longed to put his foot up! He wanted to be in his motel room, watching cable news and reading the paper. His head felt heavy. He would do anything to take off his work boot. Lewis looked to the others dining. There were almost thirty people around the table and suddenly Lewis felt as if he was dining with strangers. As if he didn't know where he was. *Am I your friend?* His head began to spin again. He got up from the table.

"I'm going to go win me some money." Lewis said.

"Take my wife," said the toolpusher, pushing his wife forward like she was choking. "She's lucky, I tell you."

"I think you need all the luck you can get." Lewis walked toward the lobby. He had to sit down. His foot. He moved to a couch in the corner. He sat down and tried to catch his breath. Tears welled in his eyes. Fucking gout, he thought. He had attacks only a handful of times a year. And each time, he felt as if the weight of his body was against him. With every step, he was grinding into the pain. He closed his eyes. He thought of Petra and wondered what she might be doing. He dozed in and out of sleep.

It was Billy's shrill voice he heard first.

"I tell you, we're goin' to see us some Indians."

Lewis opened his eyes. Billy and Worm, still in their rig clothes, were standing in the lobby. They each held longnecks in their hands and were not wearing coats.

"Yeah. Yeah," said Worm. "You'll see Indians, Billy. But let's first go win us some cash."

Lewis closed his eyes and opened them again. What were those two assholes doing here? Where was the kid? Worm should be in Lovell eating dinner with his folks and telling Will about horses. Worm and Billy headed into the casino. Lewis struggled to get to his feet, but fell back into the plush pillows of the couch. He had to roll onto his side and then onto his feet. Balling his hands into fists, he moved through the lobby, into the heart of the casino.

It took him almost twenty minutes to find Worm and Billy. Billy had already lost all his money. But Worm was up $200 on the blackjack table. They looked up from their game.

"Hey there," Billy said. We thought you boys shouldn't have all the fun. Me and Worm got to talkin' after you left and we thought, shit, we can go too. I drove," said Billy.

Worm looked away from Lew. "I got to thinkin'. Will's never left Wyomin' and I thought, hey, there's culture in South Dakota. You got Mount Rushmore, The Black Hills, Reptile Gardens, Flintstone Village…"

"And Indians," said Billy.

"Yeah. Indians. There aren't too many of those around Jeffrey City. I thought to myself, Jeanie isn't the only one who should get a vacation. I thought I'd take a vacation here with my boy. Me and Billy are takin' tomorrow off. We'll see how you like your rig tomorrow with no hands. Then maybe next time you'll take us with you." Worm took a deep drink from his bottle.

"I don't see your boy." Lewis scanned the casino.

"He's asleep. In Billy's car."

"Are you crazy?" Lewis looked through the casino to the outside doors. "It must be near 30 degrees outside."

"He's in a sleeping bag. From Cabela's. That thing's good to minus 10 degrees. He's fine."

"Yeah, and have you seen my car? It's a real nice setup," Billy chimed in.

Billy drove a motorcycle in the warmer months. In the winter, he was forced to drive a car. He kept his small Ford in impeccable condition. Most days he left it in the parking lot of the Castle Court and got a ride out to the rig, on account of the mud. When Lewis had first met Billy, he asked him what was the deal with his tattoos, the tears that marched down his face. Billy told him he got one every time a friend died in a motorcycle crash. The three tears reached the apple of his cheek. Lewis said he ought to have friends who were better drivers.

"You two are worthless," Lewis cringed at the two of them. They laughed and Lewis realized they'd had a few longnecks and god knows what else.

"I'll tell you what. Take these chips and this book of coupons. Get yourself some more drinks." Lewis handed Worm the envelope the VP had given him. "I'll check on your boy."

"You got a deal," Worm replied. "You know Lew, you ain't too bad."

"We're parked outside the casino." Billy handed his keys to Lewis. "In the lot by the tourist stand."

Lewis hobbled outside the casino's glass door. He stopped every few feet to catch his breath. It had begun to snow again. The parking lot for a Thursday was now quite full.

Lewis walked up and down the rows looking for Billy's car. He found it parked illegally, in a space reserved for the "Big Winner" of the month. His used his hand to wipe snow away from the window. He peered inside and saw empty bottles and a ring of blonde hair. Lewis opened the door and Will sat up with a start.

"I saw your dad in there. I lost my money so I thought I better call it a night."

Will nodded his head and gathered the cotton and flannel sleeping bag around him.

"You want to take a walk? Go get something to eat? Did you eat dinner? I still got some money for dinner."

Will shook his head and pointed to a bag from the same convenience store the bus had stopped at in Sundance. Will climbed out of the sleeping bag. He began to get out of the car.

"Where's your shoes?"

Will shrugged. He dug around his sleeping bag and dinner remains.

"Did you wear shoes?" The child's feet were socked.

Will began to cry. "I left 'em. I left 'em in that little house. My daddy carried me." His shoulders shook with his small grief. Lewis picked him up and shut the door of the car.

"Well, I'll carry you now." Lewis teetered unsteadily on his feet. He scanned the street before him. Casino after casino lined the block. He began to walk.

"We're going to find us a place to have a cup of hot chocolate. Do you like hot chocolate?"

"I want coffee."

"Well, I don't know about that. Does your mom let you drink that? It'll stunt your growth. My own boy, I never let him drink coffee. Now he's as tall as a weed." Lewis had to put the boy down. His foot.

Lewis stopped in front of a restaurant called Miss Molly's Parlor. A bored-looking girl in old-time dress sat behind the glass. Lewis and Will went inside.

"Table for two, please." Lewis smiled at the girl. "We need some hot drinks ASAP."

"You can have the best seat in the house," she said, pointing at a table by the window. Lewis sat Will down into one of the oak chairs. He stumbled back onto his own feet and then fell to the floor. The girl moved to his side.

"You been drinking? You need some water?"

"Nah. Football injury. Don't let this kid here fool you." He pointed a finger at Will. "He's heavy."

Will grinned. Lewis used the table to pull himself up.

"We need two hot chocolates." Lewis knew the drink was bad for his foot. He added, "And a water."

They settled into the parlor. The girl brought the drinks and a small plate of cookies for Will.

"For you and your grandpa to share."

"He ain't my grandpa!" Will called out after the girl. "I'm goin' to see my grandpa tomorrow. I'm goin' to ride a horse. We're goin' to see Indians."

"You drink that there. It'll warm you right up." Lewis studied the boy.

Will licked the cream off the top. "Why you call my daddy Worm? It ain't his name."

The question confused Lewis. He knew Worm's real name was William. He'd seen it on the log. "It's 'cause your daddy's new at the job. The man who's newest, who don't have that much experience, they're the worm. He's not really a worm, it's a joke."

"I got his name. William Zachary Taylor. He ain't a Worm."

"My boy, his name is Donald. But when he was a boy, we called him Bingo. Cause he'd always answer by calling out

BINGO when his momma and I asked him anything. BINGO! he'd say. It was a code name." Lewis started to ramble. He hadn't called Donald that in years. When he and Petra had come home that night to find their place robbed, they hadn't called the police. Bingo. They knew who did it. The next day, Lewis drove to different pawnshops in town. He bought back his own things at each one. He came home to Petra with their things piled into his truck. He hoped Donald was eating. Bingo. His son was probably in Denver right now.

Lewis held Will around his neck like a cape. He walked back into the casino. It was late and their bus was to leave in an hour. Lewis placed Will down on the couches he had sat in earlier.

"I'm going to go see if your daddy's a millionaire by now. He probably has enough to buy you a horse."

Will's face made the same surprised O it had made earlier in the day. Lewis moved back onto the floor. Lewis looked over the shoulders of the people gambling. It was mostly blue hairs and a few rough-looking folk. Up ahead was the toolpusher's wife.

"Hey, there. You lucky tonight?" he asked.

"I was. Up almost five-hundred bucks. Then I lost it all." She squinted at the table. She studied the cards trying to conjure up numbers. To see what lay beneath.

"You'll get it back. You got an hour. Listen here. I ran into some friends. Old friends. You all should go without me. I think I'll stay here. Gamble a little more. I'll drive back with them. But don't you worry. I'll be at work in the morning. Just going to see if I can retire early." Lewis grinned.

"I'll tell 'em," she replied and went back to her game.

Lewis looked around the casino. There was no sign of Billy or Worm. He went back to the lobby. Shuffling past the gift shop, the bric-a-brac was on full display. He went inside and bought Will a fake arrowhead and an Indian headdress. Will was waiting on the couch. His socked feet dangled above the ground. His face was sleepy and a ring of chocolate stained his mouth.

"An old lady there asked me if I was good luck," he said.

"What'd you say? Are you good luck?" Lewis leaned to pick him up.

"No. I ain't lucky. I told her."

"Well, Mr. Unlucky, you and me are going to get us some shuteye." He handed the child the gifts. Will put the headdress on his head and Lewis held onto the arrowhead. Will's sweatpants had no pockets. Lewis carried him out of the casino. The snow again starting to let up. Lewis tried not to slip. At the car, he worked to put Will inside the sleeping bag. He turned the engine on and settled himself into the front seat. The child slept soundly.

Lewis thought about Ned Cane. How Ned had been standing on the well-pad one morning when Lewis was the first one there. Ned was crying. He said, "I got no rights here. I got no rights here." Ned had looked at Lewis for permission, for something. Lewis had said nothing. What did he know? He was the geologist, all right. He could only make educated guesses about what was below the surface of anything. He wanted to tell Ned Cane that was the most you could expect from life. The rights to be on the surface of anything. He thought of Petra. They had been married for almost thirty years and all he knew of her was the surface. Some geology was better left untapped. Petra had looked at all of their things that day he came back from the pawnshop. She put her hand on the jumble of their cumulative lives together and sighed. "We got a lot of junk there, Lewie. I don't know why you brought it all back."

By the time Worm and Billy made it to the car they were both drunk and belligerent. Lewis woke to find Worm peeing on the car and Billy shouting about the rims of the tires. Lewis opened the door.

"You two. Get in the car. We all got to be at work tomorrow."

Worm and Billy laughed.

Billy leaned into the car. "Worm here won almost $1,000. We're rich. But we ain't seen no Indians." This thought seemed to sober him.

"I'm rich." Worm weaved into the parking lot.

Lewis stepped out. His foot creaked beneath him. He opened the back door of the car and reached in for Will. Will's body was warm and floppy. He moved around to the side of the car and opened the passenger side. He placed Will in the front seat. Air bags be damned.

"You two. Get in. I'm driving you home." It was nearly 2 a.m.

The roughnecks climbed in. Lewis hobbled to the driver's side.

"You know how to drive this baby?" Billy whimpered from the back seat. "This here's my baby."

"I can drive better then most of your friends, that's for damn sure." Lewis pulled out of the lot.

"Just don't hit any Indians," he called out. Worm was already asleep.

Lewis drove down to Gillette without the radio. He wondered if the toolpusher's wife had made back her money. What Donald had done with the money he got from selling their stuff. He wondered if Will's momma was now a married woman. He hoped the man had more spine than Worm. The snow picked up and Lewis marveled at the weird wedding of water and snow, which rained across the headlights. Ahead, across the prairie, he saw Gillette, a beacon blushing.

By the time they pulled into the Castle Court, it was near 5 a.m. Lewis would have to leave for work in two hours. That night he would drive home to Casper. To Petra. Lewis woke up the boys and again carried Will inside. Billy and Worm had rooms on the ground floor, Lewis's room was on the second floor. He needed just an hour to put his leg up. To take off his boot.

Behind the desk, the manager of the Castle Court, Mr. Khan, was already at work. Coffee brewed in the breakfast area and he looked at the men.

"Hello, Mr. Lewis. Good morning. Is it snowing again?"

"Not too bad there. I think today's going to warm right up." Lewis moved toward his room.

Billy's eyes widened. He focused on Mr. Khan and then on Worm and Lewis.

"I told you. I told you we'd see an Indian," he cried. He was drunk and tired. The tears looked like angry moles upon his face. Worm ignored him.

"Yeah. Now we've all seen an Indian," Lewis said, handing Will off to Worm. They headed for their rooms.

"I seen an Indian," mumbled Billy as he stumbled down the hallway.

Will lifted his head from Worm's shoulder, "I seen an Indian?" he asked.

"Yes," said Lewis, glancing at Mr. Khan's brown skin.

Mr. Khan was in fact, not Indian. Indeed, his family was from Karachi. He had been to India only once, to see the Taj Mahal. He had stood outside the domed peak and sighed. In that moment, he could forget what lay beneath. His gaze, instead, had remained fixed and upward.

"I'm not Indian," he called out to Lewis. "I'm Pakistani." Will's voice rang out from the hallway. "Is that better luck than an Indian?"

Lewis knew nothing of what the surface held. Or of what was underneath. He only knew how to guess, to know sometimes you got it right. Sometimes you were very wrong.

"Even better," Lewis called back, and closed the door behind him.

Dot or Feather

By the time Sindu Thyagaraja came to live in Wyoming, she was already calling herself Cindy. From the moment she left the airport in Delhi, she began practicing her new name. "My name is Cindy. Actually I'm Sindu, but Cindy is a nickname," she said to the man in the *kurta* pajamas sitting next to her on the flight to London. He snorted and continued to read a dog-eared copy of the in-flight magazine. From London to Toronto, Cindy again introduced herself, this time to the woman next to her.

"My name is Cindy. Cindy Thyagaraja. I'm on my way to Wyoming."

The woman looked at Sindu and tucked her black hair behind her ears. She wore black clothing and small gold earrings. She smelled like somewhere else. On her finger was a large sapphire.

"It's very cold there, you know. I went skiing there once years ago." The woman twisted the ring on her finger. "Make sure you have a good hat and gloves."

Sindu's thoughts moved to her suitcase. It was brand new. At first her father had brought out his old suitcase. A black hardside with his initials, "JKS," engraved on a small plate.

He had taken it to England in the sixties when he studied at the London School of Economics. The suitcase had since been used only twice: for his honeymoon trip to Kodaikanal and a conference in Delhi. When Sindu first looked at it, she saw only the viscose lining, the crumbs of murku and hot mix that had spilled out when the suitcase had flown across the sea or rumbled on the train north. It was her brother Dil who had bought her a new suitcase. A gray tweed with a rainbow strap. It had a separate vinyl name holder, and it was on this that Sindu first wrote her new name and address:

> Cindy Thyagaraja
> 112 Sego Lily Court
> Casper, Wyoming 82609
> United States of America

Sindu felt the same excitement she imagined the O'Sullivan twins or Elizabeth Allen must have felt when they began their new school terms. Only Enid Blyton could capture how she felt. Dil had always been fond of Blyton's adventure books, like the *Secret Seven* or *Famous Five* series. But Sindu preferred the boarding-school books. It was more exciting to read about new cases filled with blazers and unmarked notebooks. Sindu loved how Elizabeth and the twins left for school with tuck boxes of thickly cut sandwiches and slices of fruitcake, and flasks of tea in their satchels.

So Sindu began her preparations the minute the Rotary Club announced she had won a scholarship for a year in America. She imagined buildings with ivy creeping up the walls. She asked the man at Sweet Sweet Tailors to make her a blazer. She brought in one of her father's jackets. It was a tweed similar to that of her suitcase. He had got it in an Oxfam shop in London, and never wore it upon returning to India. The tweed made him sweat. And so Mr. Subramani looked Sindu up and down and days later delivered her own jacket. Instead of a logo on the pocket, he had embroidered a flower.

Sindu saved every spare penny to buy new clothes. She bought two pairs of jeans and plenty of T-shirts. She purchased a skirt for the journey. Her mother got her a bottle of water and a slice of fruitcake and made her sandwiches with egg and potato curry inside. The night before Sindu left she called her American host family, the Jewells. Carol Jewell answered the phone.

"Jewell residence."

"Mrs. Jewell? This is Sindu, your foreign student."

"Oh, Sin-doo, we've been expecting your call. How are you, honey?"

"Fine, thank you." Sindu didn't know whether to correct her name.

"Well, my husband, Jim, will be at the airport on Wednesday to get you. Now, Sin-doo, I was planning our meals this week. Do you eat meat? We usually have pork roast on Wednesdays."

"I eat anything, Mrs. Jewell." Sindu thought of the one time she had eaten beef. It had been at the Sheraton Hotel when her father was at a meeting. She had ordered a hamburger but managed only a few bites. The meat was chewy and raw. She had spat most of it out into a napkin. She had never eaten pork.

"Well, that's fine, dear. We have Indian friends here who are so excited to meet you. And your room is all ready. So you just have a safe flight. God bless."

"I'll see you Wednesday. Good-bye." Sindu let the phone fall onto the receiver.

She listened to the sounds of her house. She could hear the beat of Indian dance music and knew Dil was listening to film soundtracks. She heard her mother and their cook talking in the kitchen, and then the *bang bang* of the mortar and pestle. She could smell smoke. Her father was probably outside smoking cigarettes and talking to their neighbor.

She went into her room. She shared it with her Aunt Pippa, a spinster who taught physics at the university. It was Pippa who had told Sindu about the Rotary Club. Sindu looked at her open case. Her mother had put a thin layer of Indian clothes on top of her new jeans and shirts. A wool shawl was tucked into the corner. Earlier in the day, Sindu had taken out a bag of hot mix. She placed it back inside. Tears dripped onto her linen bedspread. She wiped her eyes. A new *Archie* comic lay on her bedside table. She would have girlfriends who would become chums. She would wear her blazer and her hair in a swingy ponytail like Betty Cooper's. She would meet an American boy like Archie who would think she was everything. She would order milkshakes in restaurants like Pop Tate's. She would see snow. She would become Cindy.

Cindy would later look back on her first few weeks in Wyoming as if they had happened to someone else. When she arrived at the Jewells', she found them extremely pleasant and dumb. Their house was a large ranch-style design, with a concrete patio in the backyard.

Cindy had never really known any white people. Her father had English friends from his days in London, but they only wrote or sent the occasional photograph. In Bangalore, Cindy often gave tourists directions to the Lalbagh Botanical Gardens or to Ulsoor Lake. She was amazed by their ability to travel the world. To get on a plane with a rucksack and a guidebook. She liked the women the most. Tanned, with bangles on their wrists, some of them wearing only sari slips as skirts. At times she wanted to say to them, "Take me with you. I will be your guide." But she saw herself as they saw her. Small and dark, wearing a salwaar kameez. Cindy's feet were what embarrassed her the most. Scuffed, calloused, and always covered in a fine layer of dust from the roadside. It was impossible to keep them clean.

The Jewells didn't even bother taking off their shoes when they entered the house. Fall leaves and dirt streaked their rugs. The children came in and out of the house as if it were a restaurant. It was Cindy who was at home with Carol most of the time. She went to the grocery store with Carol once a week. Carol filled the cart with frozen food and big bottles of brightly colored drinks.

"I used to cook more. But now I'm full time at the fabric store. And I take tole-painting classes twice a week."

Cindy smiled and watched as Carol placed a bag of chips on top of cans of vegetables. When she first arrived in Wyoming, Cindy thought there had been a mistake. She was expecting a Riverdale, like the one in the comic books. Instead, when she came off the plane she was nearly blown off the stairs. All around her was desert. The open spaces scared her. Where were the trees? The birds? When Carol and Jim pointed out an antelope as they drove home, Cindy felt the animal's disdain for her, although it was beautiful. It looked up and then continued eating.

When she first met Beth, Ronald, and Jimmy Jr., they had laughed at her T-shirt. Cindy had gotten it at a store known for Western fashions. It was pink. Written across it several times was "I'm too sweet!" Cindy had never really understood totally what the shirt was trying to say. But she liked that it was pink and that the letters sparkled.

"Where'd you get that shirt? If we'd known you were too sweet, we wouldn't have let you come!" Beth laughed at her own joke. Ronald and Jimmy Jr. smiled to themselves.

On her first day of school, Cindy put her hair up in a long swinging ponytail. She carefully pulled up her knee socks and put on her blazer and skirt. The day was hot. By the time Cindy got to school, sweat formed a cap around her head.

The school was not like Elizabeth Allen's Whyteleafe or even like Riverdale High. The halls were crowded and the cafeteria was flooded with fluorescent light. She went through the day virtually unnoticed.

In her math class, a thin girl in front of her turned around.

"Are you a Mo-Mo too?" she asked.

"A Mo-Mo?" Cindy didn't know what she meant.

"You know, Mormon. Those Jewells. They say Jim Jewell may have another wife somewhere!"

"Well, I've only seen the one," Cindy said. The teacher came into the class.

She looked at her shoes. They were brown oxfords. She had never owned closed-toe shoes before coming to Wyoming. When buying them at Bata she had walked around the store imagining oak dining halls and wearing a long white nightdress. She never imagined walking around the house of a maybe polygamist.

Cindy began to count down the days till she could go home. In the back of her biology notebook, she made a chart for each month and began crossing off the days. She wrote long letters home: she talked about all the fun things they did, a picnic on the mountain, her good marks, how her blazer was as good as a winter coat. What she didn't write about was how Beth never asked her to go out, how Ronald had walked in on her in the bath, and how she hated using toilet paper and hid a cup in the bathroom to wash. Carol had insisted upon a warmer winter coat, and had given Cindy an old one of hers. The coat was long and quilted. It was beige. Cindy knew she should be thankful. It was free. But she saw what the other girls had. Short parkas in pinks and blues. Hats with jolly pom-poms on the top. Gloves that stretched when your hands went into them. Carol gave her a pair of Ronald's old ski gloves. They were gray vinyl with brown stripes. Cindy's hat was a ski cap of Beth's from when she was a child. There was an appliqué of a bee on it.

The part of the Jewells' house she liked the best was their shelter for the end of the world. It was a big concrete room that took up almost all the basement. In it were metal shelves filled with canned goods, rice, first aid kits — all the things one might need in case the apocalypse came. There were easy chairs and in one corner Carol had fashioned a kind of school room. Even the curtains had chalkboards and pencils on them. Cindy escaped to the shelter at least once a day. She sat in a big overstuffed chair and sometimes tapped into the apple juice supply.

It was by chance that Cindy began to babysit. Beth had promised Mrs. Adams across the street that she would watch her girls on Friday night. As it turned out, Beth wanted to go to a football game. Carol was furious.

"I can watch them for you if you want." Cindy spoke softly over Beth and Carol's arguing. They observed her for a moment.

"Cindy...would you? I would owe you a million. See, Mom, it's all taken care of. Cindy will do it."

"Fine. But you call Mrs. Adams and be sure to walk Cindy over on Friday night. Then you can go to the game."
Cindy had seen Mrs. Adams only once. She came over rather breathlessly one morning, asking if Carol could take her girls Mari and Laura to school. Her car had a flat tire. She had long dark hair and silver rings on her fingers. She wore tall leather boots and a leather jacket. Her makeup was understated. Cindy thought she was beautiful. She wished she lived with the Adamses.

The Adams family lived in a ranch home that was better designed than the Jewells'. Instead of a front door with cement stairs leading to a walkway, the Adamses' house had a porch. Mrs. Adams had lined the porch with pumpkins and big pots of cattails. On Friday Cindy stood outside the front door. Carol was working late at the fabric store and so Beth had told Cindy to walk over by herself. Cindy rang the bell. Mrs. Adams opened the door with a wide smile.

"You must be Cindy. The girls are so excited that you are coming. We pulled down the atlas today and I showed them India. Mari here's going to be an Indian for Halloween. Well, not your kind of Indian. The kind that lives in tepees. Isn't that right, Mari?"

Mari shrugged from the stairs. She was nine and very skinny. Her hair was cut in a bowl shape around her head. It was uneven and bangs covered her eyes.

"Well. I'll show you around. This is Mari, and Laura is watching a video. We're running late. My husband had a late surgery. Now, we'll be at the house of our friends the Knolls, and then we might go out for drinks. All the numbers are on the fridge."

She moved around the house at a frenzied pace. "Help yourself to anything in the fridge. There's pop in the pantry. Laura will show you how to work the TV, and please make sure the girls are in bed by nine... 9:30 at the latest."

They left half an hour later. Dr. Adams came downstairs with wet hair and his tie untied. He nodded his head at Cindy. As Cindy shut the front door she could still smell Mrs. Adams's perfume. Cindy looked at Mari.

"Can I put on my Halloween costume?" Mari chewed her hair. Cindy paused.

"I guess so. But don't get it dirty." Mari went upstairs. She came downstairs in a brown felt dress on which her mother had strung beads on the makeshift fringe. She had a pigeon feather tucked into a headband, which she wore over the lopsided haircut. She had a Barbie in her papoose.

"I can do a war yelp. Listen. WHOOOOP!" Her face jumped with animation.

Mari made Cindy nervous. "Let's go see what your sister's doing." They moved into the den. Laura wore a too-big T-shirt and tights. Her long blonde hair was matted in the back. She also nodded at Cindy. They all watched a few minutes of cartoons, and then Mari leaned right up to Cindy's face. Cindy could feel her breath.

"I'm sorry we took your land."

"You didn't. I'm not that kind of Indian. Your mother showed you. I'm from a different place." Mari nodded and went to her room, bringing back another limp headband, the feather split in places. She handed it to Cindy.

"White people were mean to you. What tribe are you?"

"No. There are two kinds of Indians. Some wear dots, others wear feathers. You're a feather Indian. I wear a dot."

"Is your tribe in India? Were you taken away from home like Sacajawea?"

"Yes, my tribe is in India. If you want to call it a tribe. But I came here on my own, not like Sacajawea."

"Can I have a snack now?"

Cindy made her a snack of apples and peanut butter. Later they made a tambourine out of paper plates and dried beans. Mari ran around smacking it and hitting Laura on the head. She and Cindy both practiced their war yelps.

Cindy began to look around after Mari and Laura were in bed. The house was nothing like the Jewells', which was full of overstuffed recliners and fake velvet couches. Carol's own art decorated the walls. Ann-Marie Adams had good taste. Cindy felt as if she was in movie. Their couches were white leather and on the walls was real art, signed by artists. Ann-Marie had a wreath of berries above the fireplace and tasteful pictures of the girls, framed in silver. Cindy stuck her head up the fireplace. She wished that she could light a fire. The kitchen was red and white with a cookie jar shaped like a rooster. Cindy looked at all the appliances. In India they had only the basics. The red KitchenAid mixer seemed to wink at her. The juicer made her think of Saturday mornings. She imagined the Adamses around the dining-room table, pancakes on their plates, orange juice in tall glasses.

Cindy examined everything. She looked at the brand names in the pantry and noted the sparkling water in bottles. In the refrigerator were tubs of yogurt, cans of pop, and vegetables still crisp and inviting. She had never really looked into the Jewells' refrigerator. Carol was always home. Cindy mostly stayed in her room.

She began to taste a bit of everything. She ate a dill pickle and capers, cut blocks of all the cheeses in their special drawer. She peeled slices of lunch meat and stuffed them whole into her mouth. She poured herself a glass of fizzy water. She ate some of Mari and Laura's Halloween candy. She liked the small chocolate bars and the fruit- flavored lollipops. Cindy cleaned up the dishes in the sink. She didn't want Mr. and Mrs. Adams to see the evidence of her sampling.

She looked around every room. She noted what books were on their shelves, what magazines they had spread across their coffee table. She studied family pictures in front of ski slopes and at Disneyland for some clue as to how they lived. She pulled down photo albums and looked at pictures of a pregnant Ann-Marie. She noted that both Mari and Laura were ugly babies. She moved into the master bedroom. On the bed was a white crocheted bedspread. Cindy lay down. She wondered if this was how Ann-Marie felt every night. Like a princess. She wondered if Ann-Marie noticed the small water stain on the ceiling. She went into the bathroom. She smelled their soaps, looked at Ann-Marie's makeup. But she was careful not to mess anything up. Before she left the room, she squirted herself with perfume. She smelled like someone else. She was like the woman on the plane.

Cindy began to babysit most weekend nights. She added three other families to her list. Besides the Adamses there were the Meyers, the Stevenses, and the Rydells.

The Meyers were a large Catholic family with five children. The eldest two helped Cindy watch the little ones. Their pantry was sparse, and Mrs. Meyer hid most of the good snack food in an upper cupboard that Cindy dared not touch.

The Stevenses had only one child, a little boy named Jason who often cried when his parents left. The Stevenses told Cindy that no TV was allowed. But soon after they left, to muffle the cries, she would turn the TV on and let Jason watch. It was in their house that Cindy first tried red wine and ate brownies with nuts, which were on a Christmas tray.

The Rydells rarely called Cindy. Their regular babysitter was a girl from the community college. The parents were both lawyers, and Mrs. Rydell had a different last name. Their son and daughter were an energetic duo who demanded that Cindy play with them. They spent the evening jumping from card games to hide-and-seek. When they finally went to bed, Cindy lay down herself. The Rydells paid the least. They also came home drunk. Cindy sat nervously in the front seat of the car as Mr. Rydell weaved through the streets. The car's interior reeked of wine.

It was funny that as a babysitter you could know people better than if you talked to them every day. Cindy had barely exchanged a few pleasantries with most of the families, and yet she knew them. She knew the Rydells had a drawer full of sex toys upstairs. They had handcuffs and a leather outfit. She giggled to think of Mrs. Rydell in it. No wonder their children were so energetic. The Meyers, with all their religion, sometimes smoked pot in their spare room. Cindy knew the smell from the temples near her home in Madurai. The Stevenses were secretly very dirty. Their living room was all right to the casual visitor, but their refrigerator was full of rotting food. Packed inside were casseroles and vegetables that had mold on them. Cindy served Jason a plate, but never ate anything herself. They also hoarded soap and shampoo from hotels. The Adams family had three cats. Ann-Marie hated to clean their litter box. Often Cindy walked by the spare bathroom holding her nose.

Cindy didn't start taking things until nearly Christmas. At first it was by mistake. Mari asked her to hold a small plastic walrus while she went upstairs to go to the bathroom. Cindy put it in her pocket and went to drag Laura away from the TV. That night at the Jewells', she found the plastic animal. It gave her a thrill. No one knew she had it. Cindy placed it on her basement windowsill. She thought she'd give it back the next time she went over.

But she didn't. She began to take other things. She knew not to take things that would be missed. From the Meyers she took a rosary stuffed in a kitchen drawer, a train from a train set, four bath beads, and a pair of Mrs. Meyer's socks. From the Stevenses she took a book of poems from the bathroom, a chain to put glasses on, a candle shaped like a flower, and a wooden block with the letter "P" on it. The Stevenses had two hunting dogs that were kept outside. They were yellow Labs. They peered in through the glass doors, leaving fog, smudges, and mud streaks on the glass. Cindy had tried to let them in, but they jumped and nipped at her hands. She knew that they knew what she was up to.

The Rydells had so many things that Cindy wanted. Some weeks she'd take something and then switch it the next time she came over. From them she helped herself to three condoms from the bedside table (she later blew one up in her room), a pink sparkly headband, a photo of the family in Yellowstone, and a small doll that belonged in a dollhouse.

Besides the walrus, Cindy didn't take anything from the Adams house. Instead she tried on Ann-Marie's clothes, and sometimes, if it was a late evening, she'd take a bath with her bath salts. Cindy didn't know anyone with a bathtub in India. Hindus would never sit in dirty water. And it was too hot to soak in warm water. But one morning she had heard Beth and her mother talking.

"Her hair is, like, so greasy. Mom, you really should tell her to wash it. All the kids think she doesn't shower. And when she does shower, there's talcum powder all over the bathroom."

"It's the coconut oil, Beth. It's considered pretty back there. You tell the kids that."

Cindy rubbed some of Ann-Marie's shampoo into her hair. Later she dried her hair and picked up all the stray hairs on the bathroom floor. She had an hour till they came home. Downstairs, she flipped through the TV channels and then put in a home movie. It was of Laura's birth.

Cindy didn't notice the front door open. She heard Ann-Marie's voice before she saw her.

"Cindy, were they good? Did they stay up too late?" Ann-Marie looked at the TV and her own legs wide open on the screen.

Cindy sputtered, "There was nothing on TV. I thought I'd watch a tape of when the girls were younger. I...Mari told me there was a tape of her school Christmas concert."

"Yes, well, it's not that tape." Ann-Marie pressed "stop." "Here's your money. I'll call you about next weekend." Her tone was curt and tired.

At home, Cindy took out her gray suitcase. She picked up her salwaar kameezes and a sari her mother insisted she bring. All the objects she had collected in the last month lined the bottom of the case. She smelled the candle and fingered the skirt on the doll. Her latest acquisitions were Christmas ornaments from every house. She looked at the baby Jesus she had taken out of the nativity scene at the Meyers' place, the sparkling Santa from the Rydells. She held them in her hands. She held on tight.

It was after Ann-Marie caught her watching the video that Cindy began to steal from the Adamses. But this time she was bolder. She took a T-shirt that she remembered seeing Ann-Marie wearing in one of the photo albums. She took their remote control and a beater from their KitchenAid mixer and a pair of pink slippers from the back of Ann-Marie's closet. She stole toys from Mari and Laura. At night, alone at the Jewells', Cindy sat in bed wearing the T-shirt, pretending to watch TV.

Her stash was found by accident. No one really missed the things she stole. The TV remote was considered lost by Laura, and toys were always misplaced. Carol was cleaning Cindy's room. She pulled the suitcase out to vacuum under the bed. When she felt the weight, she looked inside. She recognized Beth's brush and a picture of tole-painted birds that said "Home Tweet Home" on it. The rest of the stuff was a mystery to her.

"Sin-doo, did you take these things? Why Sind-oo? What are you doing?" she later asked.

For a moment, Cindy thought of telling her it was something like out of Heidi. She was saving these things for her grandmother. But instead, she said nothing.

"I think you should think about getting a new home," said Carol.

And so Sindu left without saying good-bye to anyone. In the end Carol let Sindu keep the stuff (minus the painting and the brush) as she was too embarrassed to admit that a babysitter she'd recommended was a thief, and she certainly didn't want stolen goods in her house.

It was just past the New Year. Sindu smiled at the thought of going home. She wore her salwaar kameez and a wool shawl. In her carry-on bag was a flask of tea (non-caffeinated), a bag of chips, and Carol's nametag shaped like an apple. Because you never knew when you were going to have to reinvent yourself. You never knew if you were going to be introduced.

Washed in the Blood of the Lamb

Hast thou not poured me out as milk, and curdled me like cheese?
Thou hast clothed me with skin and flesh, and hast fenced me with
bones & sinews.

Job 10: 10-11

In the end, the transaction was fast. Simple. Clinical. Three minutes tops. There were no protests when she produced the slip of paper she had carefully typed back in America. No double looks, no consulting with anyone else. Just a look up and down and across her face by a greasy-haired Indian boy, who then inspected the cardboard boxes behind him. Each box was labeled with large fonts proclaiming their wares. Helen scanned the boxes, looking for names of medicines she recognized, but saw none.

He came to the I's and slowly pulled out a grey box. Opening it, he shuffled through boxes and foil packets with pills that were dispensed by cutting them off in strips with uneven slices. He held up two boxes of what she wanted.

"Come back. Tomorrow. Evening. We can have. This is all for now."

"Not all today? Can't you get it?"

He shook his head and handed her the two boxes.

"Tomorrow. Evening."

"Oh. Okay then." She reached out for her paper, and paid for the boxes he had. Almost a month's supply, and it was less than eight dollars! She started to walk away, then hesitated. "Can you get me this?" She made a writing motion and pointed to a notebook on the counter. He opened it. It was filled with cell phone numbers.

"Paper?" Helen asked.

The boy produced a scrap of paper from the book and Helen wrote quickly.

Xanax; she then crossed it out. Alprazolam. Alprax. She had looked up the Indian name before the trip, but hadn't typed it out. She adjusted her blonde hair to cover her face.

He held the slip. "How many you are wanting?" He asked.

"Ten." She watched him once again find the box and cut her a strip of coolness right there. She handed him fifty rupees.

"Are you Jesus's baby?"

That was the first question that Sweetlyn Moses had asked Helen after she arrived in India. They were wedged in a Suzuki Swift, and Helen rolled the window down to feel some sense of coolness. When she had gone through customs, the Indian woman in front of her was wearing her airplane blanket like a shawl. A blanket! Helen didn't want anything hot touching her skin.

"Excuse me?" She felt disoriented — was this jet lag?

"Are you Jesus's baby?" Sweetlyn laughed a squeaky laugh. Her father, Moses Moses, interrupted. They were the first Indian people Helen had ever met.

"Sweetlyn is teaching Sunday School right now — they ask the children this," he said.

"Oh. Then yes, yes I am." Helen didn't know what else to say. She had connected with the Moses family through her church back home in Wyoming, The Church Upon the Rock. For years she had seen on the bulletin board snapshots of their sister church in India, Emmanuel Triumphant Christian Church of Chennai. She and the other churchgoers had watched them build a bigger church, a school — there were even plans for an orphanage. She closed her eyes. She sat in the confined backseat of the Suzuki with Sweetlyn and her brother Abraham Moses. Abraham Moses traced circles with his finger on the glass window of the car, the streaky orbs like halos in the passing light. Moses Moses sat in front with the driver, every so often directing him in blurring Tamil.

Sweetlyn leaned into her, then turned her head to point at some sight that Helen could not make out in the night. The knot of jasmine curled around her hair crushed into Helen's mouth.

It was the same with her students back in Casper. Their bodies. They always found a way to press into her. When she leaned over their desks, a small head would ease its way back into her armpit. When waiting in line to go to lunch, an errant hand would reach out and take hers. At her desk, with its pressboard and plastic top, they would move in, standing so close, reaching, taking, wanting.

Miss. Miss. Miiisssss!

Help me.

Is this okay?

They no longer held that new baby smell. No longer held the scent of powder and bubble-gum soap. They were, for the most part, eight, some of them nine or even ten from being held back. Their bodies had not yet betrayed them. Moved into hair, breasts, voices that cracked. But they had lost that newness of childhood. Their bodies were misled through their parents. Many of them came to school in dirty clothes, with dirty heads. Food ringed their mouths. They were too young to know they smelled. That they needed to brush their teeth every day. Too young to know she found it hard to like them. Too young to know it was rude to ask, *What's wrong with your skin?*

The Moseses did not ask anything about what was wrong with Helen's skin. If they thought anything of it, they did not say. Instead, after arriving at their house, after meeting Moses Moses's older daughter Hosanna, Moses Moses took Helen aside to explain about Abraham.

His wife, Joy Bell, had died in childbirth. They were on a mission trip in Kerala. There was botched midwifery. Abraham Moses may look normal — but as Moses Moses explained, he was like a tube light.

"It takes a bit for him to turn on. His mind flickers. He looks good. But not right in the head. Not 100 percent," he said.

Helen didn't care two bits about Abraham Moses or about the Emmanuel Triumphant Christian Church of Chennai. She was here for the medicine.

"I wouldn't have known," she lied politely. Then asked if she could lie down.

The trip to India, to be a medical tourist, was something that had come to Helen almost six months ago. Helen Clark had bad skin. She would puzzle over photos of herself at fifteen, right before her peach skin had moved into being red and angry, before it became pocked and rough. In later years, she managed to only be in the background of photos. When she posed with her third grade class each year, she always lurked on the margins. She grew her blonde hair long with sweeping bangs to cover her face. She went on every antibiotic, every cream that promised a miracle on late night TV, and then, in desperation, the strongest medicine for acne, Accutane. This was the miracle. She did the five-month treatment, and for almost a year her skin cleared. Her face, while pocked, was free of the red pustules that made making eye contact with anyone impossible.

But after a year, her skin began again to break out. Helen went on birth control pills, even though she hadn't slept with anyone since college. She was almost thirty-one, and she looked like a teenager.

She tried again to go back on Accutane, but the prescription was over $500 a month. Besides that, she had to go monthly to the doctor for an exam, take pregnancy tests before the next prescription was doled out. The cost for the months of treatments was almost $3,500. She couldn't afford it. Once was all she could do. Insurance told her it was cosmetic, so it couldn't be covered.

"Cosmetic? You don't understand — my face hurts! It's more than bad skin!" She cried to a woman from her insurance company.

"You want my advice?" The woman on the line paused and then whispered, "Get it online."

Hosanna and Sweetlyn Moses were almost in their mid-twenties and not married. They explained to Helen that it was more complicated, on account of the two of them were so close in age, and because the pool of eligible Christian men was smaller.

But Sweetlyn, who was younger at twenty-three, was almost engaged to Mathias Davids. She told Helen that in just weeks, their banns would be announced in church. The engagement would soon be formalized.

Sweetlyn told her Mathias was an engineer, and to Helen's surprise, Sweetlyn was too.

"Do you love him? Do you mind having an arranged marriage? Have you kissed?" They sat on plastic covered furniture in the Moses's living room.

Hosanna and Sweetlyn laughed at being asked these questions.

"It's a love marriage! I mean, Appa set it up, but I could have said no. Mathias and I go out most nights — for ice cream and juice. I know him."

"I know, it's just strange for me," said Helen. The cup of tea in Helen's hand had developed a skin on the surface. She dipped her finger into the cup and tried to move the skin away. She wished Moses Moses would arrange a marriage for her. She could imagine him sweeping into Casper, Wyoming and finding her a suitable match. Then she could rest. She could sit with her skin and not think twice about her face — as Moses Moses would make sure the match would stick. She was now thirty-two and just longed for her wedding to be over so she could focus on a house, on having children. Her own parents showed little interest in Helen. Instead, they doted on her sister Laura's three small children.

Hosanna looked her in the eye and said, "I know what you Americans think. It's bad — but in our country we pee in public and kiss in private, and in your country, you pee in private and kiss in public. It's just different." Hosanna seemed pleased at her assessment.

Some of us don't kiss at all, is what Helen wanted to say. She arranged her hair over her face and looked away.

After talking to the insurance lady, Helen had spent that very evening looking online for her drugs. Sure enough. There were drugs to be had. From pharmacies in Canada. In Mexico. And from India. The brand from India flashed up in site after site. But many sites did require prescriptions. It was when reading a blog that documented in great detail an Arizona teen's report of skin that had changed from a mess to clear, that she saw someone's comment. How easy it was to get Accutane, which was called Isotretinoin, in India. *I wish I could just hop on a plane!* said Mike from Iowa.

In bed, Helen thought about it. School had just begun, but as a teacher, she had a nice long Christmas break. How much did a plane ticket to India cost? Where would she stay? Surely it would be cheaper than going through a doctor here. And dammit, if I have to spend money at all, I'd rather spend it on a trip than giving it to the man, she thought. It was in the morning that Helen knew something else. That she wanted to live a more adventurous life. She wanted to travel. And going to get medicine was as good a reason as any.

Moses Moses was nervous about letting Helen out of his sight. For her two weeks in India, he mapped out a complete itinerary of all that Chennai and the surrounding areas had to offer.

"You must go to Fort St. George. Yes. And see Marina beach. Sweetlyn and Hosanna will take you to T. Nagar. There you can get frocks. You can go to Mahabalipuram. No problem, not far at all. DakshinaChitra...and if there is time Pondicherry, and of course, you must come to our church," said Moses Moses.

She had told the Moseses she was just here to see the sights. That their monthly missives to The Church Upon the Rock had filled her with the spirit of the Lord. Filled her with the desire to see India, the darkest continent. Or was that Africa?

Back home in Wyoming, Helen did go to The Church Upon the Rock every Sunday. It was something to do. Because of her skin, she hated to go out. But at church, she turned her burden into a blessing.

"We must look past the superficial!" She would rock and

sway during her own testament in church. "The Lord does not give us anything we cannot bear. I am of the flesh of Jesus! Did God not say, 'For you created my inmost being; you knit me together in my mother's womb. I praise you because I am fearfully and wonderfully made.'" Helen would then sit down smiling, to show the congregation her skin was no big thing, not like having a birthmark, not like being retarded.

Abraham Moses was dispatched to escort Helen everywhere. Moses Moses himself had a job, as did Sweetlyn and Hosanna. So in the daytime, other members of Emmanuel Triumphant Christian Church of Chennai would come and take her around. But between church well-wishers, Helen was left at home with Abraham and the servants. Helen didn't know how to ask where to get medicine. But her question was soon answered when she had a bout of diarrhea on her fourth day in India. Abraham was sent to the medical shop around the corner, and came back with some sort of stomach antibiotic.

On her sixth day in India, Helen asked Abraham if he could help her.

"Can you take me to the same shop? For medicine?" She spoke loudly and made many hand gestures. "I need medicine."

Abraham Moses was tall and you couldn't tell by looking at him that he wasn't quite right in the head. His hair was thick and black, he had a trim moustache and bright white teeth. He dressed in Western clothes — khaki pants and button-down shirts, but at night he and Moses Moses would change into lungis and undershirts. He was slim, while Moses Moses had a belly that strained his thin shirts. Abraham Moses loved motorcycles and carried around a toy motorcycle with him at all times. In the Moses family's living room was a cupboard full of knickknacks — stuffed bears, cheap crystal vases, silk flowers, Reader's Digest condensed books, and Abraham's toy motorcycle collection.

"Yes. Yes," he said. "Medicine."

The only other people at home were the two servants. One was a young girl who looked to Helen to be a teenager. She was thin and giggled every time she served Helen food. The other one was an old woman. The first morning after Helen arrived, she was startled by the sight of her at breakfast. Her skin was a bright yellow. It was as if she had developed jaundice overnight.

"Is she okay?" she asked Hosanna.

"Oh yes. It's turmeric. It's good for the face. For the skin. Makes it lighter. More fair. It gets rid of hair." The servant's yellow specter loomed over the table.

But hers weren't the only skin problems Helen noticed. India had its share of skin problems. People with faces pitted with smallpox scars. Beggars with flesh eaten away by leprosy. (Oh! What would The Church Upon the Rock think of this! Real leprosy!) Milk-white patches of vitiligo splotching the dark Indian skin. In her first days in India, from the airport to the local market, Helen saw so many with vitiligo — women with hands as white as her! But dark skin itself was a burden, as everyone wanted to be fairer.

When in auto rickshaws and outside shops, she felt drawn to the blue-skinned Krishna. His blue face smiled on decals, he merrily played the flute in pictures. How funny it was to have a god that was blue, how funny that he wasn't in their own perfect image.

The Emmanuel Triumphant Christian Church of Chennai was big on hymns. Back home in Wyoming, the music of her church consisted of a guitar and keyboard. The congregation mumbled through the upbeat contemporary hymns. But at The Emmanuel Triumphant Christian Church of Chennai, the congregation sang. And they sang.

Are you washed in the blood,
In the soul cleansing blood of the Lamb?
Are your garments spotless? Are they white as snow?
Are you washed in the blood of the Lamb?

Lay aside the garments that are stained with sin,
And be washed in the blood of the Lamb;
There's a fountain flowing for the soul unclean,
O be washed in the blood of the Lamb!

The women of the church wore bright saris, and Helen though to herself that she must get one before she left India. She felt rather proud of how cheaply she had managed to make the whole trip. Besides the plane ticket, which was just over a thousand dollars, she had spent almost no money. She had driven to Denver to start her trip, as flying out of Wyoming added hundreds onto a ticket, and the small prop plane that departed from Casper made you sick (this from Ms. Phelps who taught first grade). In fact, she was almost making money! When The Church Upon the Rock knew she was going to darkest India on a mission, they had raised money for her! They had a bake sale and a car wash, then gave her the collection plate from the Sunday before she left. They were waiting for a slideshow when she returned, for her testament. Yes, Helen planned to do a little shopping before she left India.

After Helen had pocketed the Xanax, she thought about how she could sneak out the next day to pick up the medicine. She needed a five-month supply, which was no small number of pills.

"Are you sick?" Abraham, who had been standing on the makeshift sidewalk, asked Helen this with such clarity that

Helen wondered if he was indeed sick in the head.

"I have bad skin. This medicine, you see this?" She held up the two boxes. "This will make it better. I'll be fair and lovely." She motioned to her face. The night before, Sweetlyn had shown Helen her tube of fairness cream.

"I put this on at night, and then my skin will be like you," she said.

"Like me?" Helen touched her own face.

"Yes, white," said Sweetlyn. "You know, fair. Mathias isn't dark, so I need to be careful." Sweetlyn and Hosanna took umbrellas with them every time they left the house. At first Helen thought that it might rain, but then realized they feared the sun might make them dark.

Abraham smiled and pointed to a fairness cream ad that hung on the side of the shop. "He who was revealed in the flesh was vindicated in the spirit, beheld by angels, proclaimed among the nations, believed on in the world taken up in glory. 1 Timothy. Chapter 3, Verse 16." He laughed and fingered his motorcycle.

Sweat trickled down her forehead. Helen was itching to take a pill. Not the skin medicine, but a Xanax. They walked past a butcher shop. Chickens were stacked up in wire cages, goat carcasses hung from hooks in the storefront. A stream of blood trickled between their feet.

"You don't know what it's like to look like this, to be a monster. To look like that." She pointed at the skinned goats, then arranged her hair like a halo around her face. "You can't know."

"Very pretty," said Abraham, looking down at his motorcycle and spinning the wheel.

It surprised her to learn that once Moses Moses had married off Sweetlyn and Hosanna, he was planning to get Abraham married.

"But to who?" Helen asked Hosanna. Helen was already amazed to know that Hosanna herself was going to be married. She seemed, at twenty-five, like an old lady. She wore her thick hair in a tight bun, and had large glasses that did nothing for her face. Sweetlyn, on the other hand, often wore her hair loose or with flowers strung through it. She wore clothes the colors of confection, and always had a wrist full of color-coordinated bangles.

"To whom? To a girl. Appa hasn't found her yet, but once we are married, and if Appa dies, who will watch over Abraham? He needs a wife. The girl will be taken care of." Helen's eyes flicked around the room, and while the Moses family was not rich, they were comfortable. She understood. It would be a poor girl grateful to live in some sort of comfort.

"But, would she be happy?"

"Happy? This is a good home. We are a good family. Besides, Appa took him to the doctor. Everything is fine. He can consummate the marriage. That part is normal. All of that is working." She motioned to Helen's crotch.

Helen thought of Abraham making love. It was more awkward than thinking of herself doing it. She wondered if he would have the plastic motorcycle with him.

As it turned out, Helen didn't go back to the pharmacy the next day or the day after. Instead she went from historic site to historic site. To Fort St. George, which she found dull. Who cared what the British did? She was glad to be American, to be well out of it. The Marina was a crowded dirty beach with creaky amusement rides tottering on the sand. And T. Nagar was a crush of people all buying, buying, buying. Helen bought two saris for herself, some soapstone elephants, and some salwaar kameezes — one red, the other green.

At DakshinaChitra, a folk art center, she hit the tourist wall. It was hot. She was tired. And the cheap pair of new leather sandals she was wearing hurt her feet. Helen sat in the reproduction of a Chettinad House while Sweetlyn, Hosanna, Abraham, and Mathias took in the shadow puppet show, looked at the Tanjore paintings, and looked at all the Tamil Nadu and Kerala house reproductions.

She was embarrassed to find Mathias good looking. She didn't think she liked dark-skinned men, but Mathias was so accommodating, so quick to make sure she was comfortable. If he noticed her face, he did not show it.

"That suit is very nice," he said. The others had gone off to buy tender coconuts.

Helen was wearing her new green outfit. He put his hand up and lightly touched her hair. Helen's face was always a red color, but she blushed all the same. Helen wasn't obese, but she was fat. She knew it, but in the long shirt, she felt slimmer, lighter. She justified her eating by thinking if her face looked bad, she might as well give up. She had now been on the Accutane for three days. She planned to join Weight Watchers when she got back to Wyoming.

Mathias was shorter than her, but was strong, and dressed well. He had a gold pen in his buttoned-down shirt pocket, wore clean black pants. He wore a gold chain-link bracelet on his wrist.

As she waited, Helen realized something. She was pretty in India. She could be fat. She could be acne-ridden. But she was white. And, as Sweetlyn explained, to be fair was everything. All around Chennai were massive billboards for sari shops, for films, for jewelry stores. There were even advertisements for medical tourism — hospitals that promised a foreign ward, quick knee replacements and back surgeries. She had even seen an ad in the local tourist magazine that promised wombs for infertile couples from the West. All the women in the ads, though dark-haired and vaguely Indian, were as white as she was. She had thought as she ate ice cream at the beach or when she walked up and down the floors of Pothys sari shop that people were looking at her skin. They were, but not for the flaws, but for its white perfection. She felt the power of America, the power of being white. She might be ugly in Casper, Wyoming. But in India, she was the one people wanted to pose in pictures with, she was the one getting all the looks. Helen wondered if she should look for a teaching job here.

All around DakshinaChitra, there were local craftsmen showing their weaving and painting, there were demonstrations of kolam art and dancers giving a performance. The group came back to get Helen, but told her that Sweetlyn wanted to find the man who had a parrot that would tell your fortune before they left. Or, as Hosanna explained, the bird picked a card that told your fortune.

"But the Lord is the only person that can determine your fortune," Hosanna said.

"But God may speak through the parrot, so we'll go," said Sweetlyn.

The parrot told Hosanna that she would have a dispute with a neighbor, but she would be in the right. It told Abraham to watch out for the rains, which was strange, since it was December, and they had just finished for the year. For Sweetlyn, she was told to eat jalebis and to avoid milk. Mathias was to watch any and all business transactions for the next two weeks, and for Helen, the parrot simply told her good news was in store.

"Maybe you're getting married!" said Sweetlyn. She looked dusty in the sun. But Helen realized that is was just talcum powder on her skin, which made her ashy in the light.

By the time Helen got her medicine, she only had another few days in India. On her bed were boxes of Accutane. She had been on the medicine for a week, and so far felt no side effects. India is the place to be on this medicine, she thought. Back home, living over a mile high, her skin dried into scaly flakes. When she had been on it before, she bled out of every orifice. Her nose, when she went to the bathroom. She carried lotion and lip balm in every pocket.

When she had gone to get the rest of the medicine, Abraham had tagged along as usual. There was a big cricket game on, and she knew he wanted to stay home.

"Does, Appa…" Sometimes Abraham seemed to stutter. "Does Appa know you are not well?"

"Let's not worry him! He'll feel bad. He is my host, we can't tell him." They walked quickly, only pausing with a large group of men pressed against the window of an electronics store, all of them straining to watch the game inside.

With all her medicine bought, Helen felt celebratory. She also was itching for a drink. When she had arrived at the Moseses, she had brought them a bottle of duty free whiskey. Moses Moses smiled and pretended it was too much, and now after almost two weeks with them, she realized they were, like many of the Emmanuel Triumphant Christian Church of Chennai, teetotalers. Helen didn't consider herself a big drinker, but lately she had spent too many nights alone in her condo, watching reality TV shows and drinking boxed wine. Glass after glass, till she fell into bed and into deep sleep.

Helen knew being on the medicine meant she shouldn't drink as much, but she felt giddy. She had spent almost two weeks in a third world country! Much more than any other teacher in her school had done. They mostly took off for long weekends in Vegas or Branson, Missouri.

In the same tourist magazine that advertised wombs for rent, she had read about The Raj. A five-star hotel that actually offered medical tourist packages. Once one left the foreign ward of various hospitals, you could relax in five-star comfort at The Raj. It was an old colonial building, repurposed to be "Indian." They had doctors on call. They boasted a Palm Court and served Western food. But they also would bring you ayurvedic concoctions that were sure to speed up the recovery process. They had a pool by which a nurse would come change your dressings poolside. They also had a nightclub and bar called Fedora.

Fedora was not technically attached to The Raj. It was in a low building next to the hotel. There were no windows, and a line of trees made a shelter from the chaos of the Nungambakkam High Road.

Sweetlyn and Hosanna could not be persuaded to come out with Helen, and for a moment, Helen worried that Abraham would be forced to come along. But since Helen was leaving in a few days, Moses Moses had relaxed a bit. She was going to a five-star hotel, and Moses Moses rationalized she would be safe there — it was full of other foreigners. Helen assured him she would be safe, that she had a thin money belt she would wear underneath her salwaar pants.

As Helen was getting ready and putting on her red salwaar kameez, Sweetlyn watched her dress.

"Mathias sometimes goes to the Raj. For work. But I don't like it. I like the Breeze Hotel," she said.

They had eaten at the all-you-can-eat buffet at the Breeze several nights before. It was a nice Indian run hotel, but no five-star. Helen could tell Sweetlyn was tempted to go with her, but only liked to be where she was comfortable.

Helen paid her auto driver and walked up to the club. When Helen entered Fedora, she was glad the Moses sisters and brother had stayed home. The sheer volume of the noise was raucous and disorienting.

Boom Boom. The loud bass of a techno song made Helen's head pulse. She smoothed her hand over her new salwaar kameez. The bar was crowded, mostly full of Indian men. But a few slim women in Western dress were scattered around the club. Helen went to the bar. While walking, she unconsciously moved her hair to partially veil her face. It was quite dark inside the club, and she felt a safety in the dim lighting.

"Jack and Coke," she said to the bartender.

The bartender nodded and set to making the drink. Helen turned her back to the bar, and watched the dance floor. The inside of Fedora had low ceilings. And everything was awash with purple velvet. From the squat ottomans to the wallpaper, a grape tinge dominated its entire decor. Beside the bar was a small sitting area, and a black-and-white checked dance floor.

"Thank you." Helen took her drink and sipped it quickly through a thin straw. There was no ice in the glass, and the coke tasted sweet and syrupy.

Helen rearranged her hair and tapped her foot to the music. In Casper, there were few places to dance. There was a cowboy bar on the outskirts of town. On the weekends it was packed with roughnecks and ranch hands, all with money to spend. Helen actually enjoyed going there, which she did once a year with other teachers. Watching a couple two-step made her a little melancholy. She felt like she was watching the hands of a clock go round and round. But to see a couple move, so in synch, so close, always made her want to be on the dance floor.

The DJ at Fedora switched up the music, and a song from the nineties blasted out. Helen remembered dancing to it at her prom. Back when she thought her skin troubles would be over when she hit eighteen.

"What's the best thing I can do for my skin?" she had asked her family doctor then.

"Turn eighteen," was his laughing reply.

Helen finished the last of her drink and put it down on the bar. She ordered another. And another. And by the time Bryan Adams came on, she was drunk.

It was that song from *Robin Hood*. She hadn't seen the movie, but for one summer, the song had been the backdrop for trips to Alcova Lake, picnics in the Big Horns. Couples began to fill the floor, and Helen staggered out onto the dance floor. She swayed with the music and sang along softly, her eyes closed.

She felt a hand on her waist and shoulder.

"Hell-en. Hell-en."

Helen opened her eyes to see Mathias. He was sweating and his breath smelled of whiskey. They began to dance. He kept a respectful distance, and moved her around the floor like a pawn. Up and down. Up and down along the square checks. He felt sorry for her. She could feel it. The way he looked over to the group of men he was with. The way he moved her in jerky motions. Maybe he hadn't thought she was pretty that day at DakshinaChitra.

Helen laughed. "I like this song." Her flip-flops scraped along the floor and she moved ineptly.

Mathias was quiet and the song merged into one with a quick beat. She couldn't tell if the song was Indian or Western. The drum beat was syncopated, the sound of a sitar whined. The beat picked up and the couples around them broke into free dance. Mathias's friends came onto the floor. Helen thought of the dancers they had seen that day at DakshinaChitra. There, at first, Hosanna and Sweetlyn had barely acknowledged the dancers who demonstrated their South Indian traditional dance out in the dusty sun. They wanted to get to the parrot and its prophecies.

As they had crossed the courtyard outside the Chettinad House, Helen had stopped to look at the dancers. They were doing Bharatanatyam. Their posture was straight and upright, like a lodgepole pine. They wore bells around their ankles. Their hands seemed to have no bones the way they bent and moved. Their eyes moved back and forth almost like they were laughing at her. Hosanna and Sweetlyn came back to Helen.

"Their bodies are supposed to be like a dancing flame," Hosanna said. "Like fire — they move like fire." Hosanna pointed at the dancers.

Sweetlyn took Helen's hand.

"Are you Jesus's baby?" Sweetlyn asked again.

"Yes…well, I don't know," Helen said.

"Then you are Satan's." And Sweetlyn had dropped her hand and walked away.

At Fedora, Helen stopped for a minute and caught the beat. She moved her feet in the same movement that she had seen at DakshinaChitra. She was sweating and she felt the drinks in her stomach. But still she spun and turned, moving her hands like she was handing somebody something.

And now she felt Mathias's hand upon her waist again. He rubbed her stomach, and Helen still swiveled. When she felt his hand on her breast, she stopped for only a second. His hand moved up and down, cupping her breast and moving down her legs. She kept dancing.

This was, apart from an oily ayurvedic massage she experienced a week ago, the only contact she had felt in so long. Sweetlyn and Hosanna were lucky. They didn't have to waste night after night going to bars, scanning who was there and trying to look like they were having a good time. They could sit passively, do nothing, and still be married by twenty-five. *I am on fire*, she thought. She didn't think of Sweetlyn or of anyone. She just thought how good it felt to be touched. How good it felt to feel comfortable in her own skin.

She turned around, still moving to the beat, and from behind, Mathias wrapped his arms around her in a sort of embrace. They moved together as the music escalated. It was when she felt his hand clumsily go under her shirt that Helen stopped him. His hand stopped at her money belt, which acted as a sort of chastity belt.

"Don't," she said.

Mathias put his hands up and continued to dance. His friends around him laughed. The money belt had become loose, and she felt it ring her hips like a bangle. She held her stomach and left the club, trying to adjust it.

In the parking lot, two auto rickshaw drivers approached her.

"Madam. Madam. Where you are going Madam?"

"Need ride? Safe. 100 percent." They crowded her.

Helen didn't negotiate. She climbed into one and told him the Moseses' address.

He turned around, "Very long distance. Two-hundred rupees."

She knew the house was less than ten minutes away. Hosanna had told her not to pay more than sixty rupees. She was getting screwed.

"Fine. Fine," she said.

The driver didn't register surprise at her lack of negotiation. He started the engine and the auto began to putt putt away from Fedora. Helen put her hands down her pants and adjusted her money belt.

There was one lone light on outside at the Moseses'. Helen paid the driver and watched him make a turn in the driveway. At the door, she peered in through the wrought iron grill. She hated to wake the house, but she had no key. She could see a dim light coming from the kitchen. She called out through the bars.

"Hello! Hello!" Her voice was a sharp whisper.

From the darkness she heard someone coming. Abraham came to the door, holding the keys in one hand, the plastic motorcycle in the other. He put down the motorcycle and opened the door. The servants must have been asleep.

"Sorry Abraham. It was late, I didn't know who was up," she said.

Abraham said nothing, but locked the door behind her and picked up his motorcycle.

"Harley Davidson," he said.

He was wearing a lungi and nothing else. The outside light cast a dim shadow on his bare chest. His skin was smooth and clear. He was surprisingly lean and muscled. When Mathias had touched her at the club, she could forget it was wrong for a moment. She was the tourist. The foreigner. She didn't know the customs, it wasn't her fault.

But this was her fault. Because she wanted to feel his skin. And because she knew the power of her skin. She remembered what Hosanna had said. The doctors said he was normal. He could consummate a marriage. *All of that is working.*

They stood in the entryway, and Abraham again repeated, "Harley Davidson."

Helen ran her hand over his chest, and around his back. She pulled him close to her. He smelt of coconut oil and toothpaste. She began to kiss him. Because she could.

Abraham awkwardly hugged her. Helen moved her hand over his back, rested her head on his shoulder. She kissed him harder.

Plink. The motorcycle hit the tile floor. The toy bounced and rested near her foot. She continued to hug him, then pulled back to look at him.

Abraham took his hands and moved them up to her face. He cupped her cheeks, and Helen recoiled. No one touched her face. She jumped back with a start.

"No, no, not my face," she said.

Abraham didn't react. He squatted down to the floor and picked up the toy.

"Harley Davidson," he said again.

Her skin burned. She had crossed borders for her skin. To save it.

"Yes, that's a Harley," she said.

She turned and went up the stairs to her room. She bolted the door and switched on the light. The tube light flickered then came on. She went to unclip her belt when she saw her hands. They were bright pink — her palms a washed-out red. Helen untied her salwaar pants and saw the red all over her legs. She stripped down and saw her whole body was covered in red. Was it a rash? Was it the drinks? Helen rubbed her leg. In the mirror, she could see her face and feet were the only thing not covered with the stain.

She kicked the salwaar aside, and then noticed the white drawstring was also red. It was the vegetable dye. It covered her body. It covered her skin.

In the bathroom, Helen turned on the shower, not bothering for the water to heat up. Helen rocked underneath the water's spray. She picked up a terra cotta scrubber. Its rough surface was pocked and puckered. She rubbed it into her flesh again and again. The water swirled pink below her feet. She thought of the blood of the lamb, no the goat, that day in the market, how it had trickled between them.

Are your garments spotless? Are they white as snow?
Are you washed in the blood of the Lamb?

Under the water, her raw scrubbed flesh blushed and reddened under her futile rhythm. Helen stood trembling for her sins of the flesh, for her the sin of her skin.

White Wedding

My sister was marrying white. This was not a surprise to me. Growing up, we mostly had white dolls (we didn't like the black ones presented to us by well meaning friends). We went to school with white people. Our friends who came over to the house for barbeques and parties were white. Even our church was all white. And to be fair to Asha, it had happened in our family before. My mother had married white as well. And to be even fairer, at the last Census, Wyoming was 93.9 percent white. We fell into the 1.5 percent that was Other. Neither here nor there. We were used to white people.

But Asha had met her fiancé Tom not here, but far away from Wyoming in New York City, which is 44.7 percent white. And my mother met my father in Illinois, where they both had been graduate students. So although Asha and I fell into a grey area of being neither white nor Indian, we certainly had the cards stacked against us when it came to white people.

Asha lived in New York City and came back to Wyoming once a year, if even that. While home, she spent time marveling at the ease in which you could move from Point A to Point B, the lack of organic food available, and how *big* everything seemed — from the prairie to the size of steaks that graced her dinner plate. Secretly I think she liked coming home. She liked the mall and how everyone knew us. It also gave her an excuse to eat at the Red Lobster and Applebee's, since they were some of the nicest restaurants in town. There was a persistent rumor that an Olive Garden was opening, but we had watched for years, and never saw so much as a foundation being poured.

Asha was getting married in two days, and we were days into what she had dubbed on her wedding invitations "Western Week!" Tonight was a chuckwagon dinner, and everyone had been driven out to a location, then been moved less than a quarter of a mile in a covered wagon to a campsite. A catering company, whose name I never caught but whose logo was a pair of interlocking B's that looked like a brand, served up thick burgers, hot dogs, grilled corn, and chicken that still was pink on the inside. For dessert they gave us cool slices of watermelon.

The whole wedding party plus all the out-of-town guests were here for this Western extravaganza. Many of them had bought cowboy boots in town earlier in the day. Some of the men sported Western shirts that I felt were being worn in a way that made me unsure of what they were saying about Western life. There was something about snap-button shirts paired with thick black horned-rimmed glasses that made me suspicious. Even Tom's father had purchased a hat. A black wool Stetson that made him look like he was going to rob our wagon train at any moment.

Only my dad and I held back. We both kicked at the campfire and hoped the fire pit was deep and well made. We'd had a wicked summer of wildfires.

When the dinner was done, a man hired to look like a cowboy stepped in front of the fire. He had a handlebar mustache and a red bandana around his neck. He wore boots and a stained hat. I'd seen him before at the bar that I frequented with my friends Valentine and Amy. I knew he actually worked for the post office. I had seen him do karaoke in his postal uniform. He blew into a pitch pipe and then began to sing:

Some trails are happy ones,
Others are blue.
It's the way you ride the trail that counts,
Here's a happy one for you.

He then informed us it was time to circle the wagons, and we all piled back in for the short ride home.

I lived with my father in a house near the bottom of Casper Mountain. Our house mostly looked onto other houses, but we could see the mountain. In the fall, aspens turned and appeared like a yellow bruise on the mountain's green-brown face.

My father and I had come to a sort of routine over the past two years. I woke early and just before 5 a.m., I'd make coffee for him. Then I would get ready to go to the coffee shop. Sometimes I would make him a lunch if he was in town, and leave it on the counter in an insulated bag. I liked driving through town when almost no one else was up. I'd get to the coffee shop and turn on the machines and start brewing large airpots of coffee. By 6 a.m., everything would be ready, and the stream of regulars would come in. For some people, I'd start making their drinks the minute I saw their car pull up outside. Even with the altitude, I could make the milk in a cappuccino foam into stiff white peaks.

By 9 a.m., the store would have slowed down, with most people settled into their desks at work, paper cups full of coffee and sickly sweet lattes in their hands. Right after 9, a group of geologists came in. They were all older men, but not quite at retirement. They had been through boom, then bust, now boom again. They had earned it to sit and drink $1 coffees and talk shop. If the store was quiet, I would make a coffee and sit with them. With what happened with my mother, I'd earned the right to sit at their table. To listen. We all had war stories around that table. We'd all had loss.

When Asha first mentioned getting married in Wyoming, I laughed.

"Get married in New York," I said. "That's where all your friends are."

"I want to get married in Casper. In a tent near the mountain."

I saw about a million and one reasons why this was a bad idea. The first being that anyone having an outdoor wedding in Wyoming was nuts. If it wasn't the snow, it was the wind. We had had Fourth of Julys with snow. And the thought of a tent with no wind buffer made me snort.

I also thought about how hard it was to get people from outside in. We had one small airport, but it was dinky. I imagined most people would fly to Denver, then drive.

"Get married in Jackson. It's pretty there. People love the Tetons. They love the antler arches in the town square. There are nice restaurants. There are shops. People like that Western shit. It's close to Yellowstone. People will see bison and bears..."

"Lucky, I don't want to get married there. I want to get married in the same church I was baptized in, in the same church I was confirmed, and in the same church that mom's funeral was in." Her exasperation with me was always tempered the first day or so that she came home, and then it would come out.

"Right," I said. There wasn't much more to say. But Casper

was the Oil City of the Plains. Our mountain was small, our town scrappy. It wasn't the West people were expecting. Most cowboys wore baseball hats. I felt like we were letting them down.

When I finished work in the early afternoon, my pockets would be stuffed with dollars and quarters from the tip jar. I'd store up a week's worth of tips in a mason jar in my room, then take it to the bank on Fridays.

In the summer and into the fall, when I finished work I'd drive up the mountain. I had a thinking spot on the back side of the mountain. I'd even fashioned a little stool out of a fallen log. Usually I would sit there getting blown over. In the winter, I'd sometimes snowshoe in. With so much horizon, I felt I could think.

And this is how I spent my days. The coffee shop. Driving aimlessly. Making dinner if my dad was in town and not on a rig. Then at night going out with Valentine or Amy. We rotated between three bars. The Wonder Bar if we wanted beers, Sidelines if we were hungry, as they had free buffalo wings at Happy Hour, and if we were feeling posh, we went to Vintage, which was sort of a wine bar.

When people asked me at the coffee shop if I missed my job or was I going back to school, I answered honestly.

"No. You know me. I love being here. I don't think Casper's so bad."

And it was true. I was still trying to figure out why almost everyone I knew from high school had left. How I had become the townie. At Christmas and Thanksgiving breaks, I smiled when I ran into old classmates.

"Yep. Still here....No, I left school....No plans to go back...She died two years ago...yeah, it was sad..." And the conversation went on.

Asha came home two weeks before the wedding. She borrowed my truck, and drove around meeting with photographers, caterers, and the priest who was marrying them. I continued working. I even made lattes for her New York friends when they started arriving.

After Asha had been home a week, she came into my room. I was reading. Even though I had dropped out of my PhD program, I still liked to read.

"Lucky, I've been thinking about you," she said.

"Good. I'm glad to know you do," I said.

"Lucky. I worry for you. You live with dad. You don't date. You work at the coffee shop. What are you doing?"

"Well, all of those things. And I date," I said, a little defensively.

"Seriously. When were you last on a date?"

I thought a moment and knew it had only been a month ago. A guy I met at The Wonder Bar asked me to go dancing, as I loved to two-step. What he failed to tell me was that the dance was at a muzzleloading convention, for the final banquet. We arrived at a chain motel and when we went into their ballroom/convention center, it was filled with Davy Crocketts and a sort of Pioneer-woman-meets-Renaissance wench. My date and I were the only people in non-period costumes. That changed midway when my date bid on a mountain man coat at the dinner auction. He wore the leather-fringed number for the rest of the night. He had drunk his beer from a pewter horn, which he also had won. I had called my dad from the lobby to pick me up.

"You know what you are?" Asha grabbed my hand to make me listen.

"An American?" I made a lame joke at the question we had been asked so many times: *What are you?*

"No, Lucky, you're like a prairie dog."

"I tunnel underground and am cute?" I laughed.

She paused. "No, Lucky, you're like one of those prairie dogs you see by the side of the road. When you're driving. The ones that pause there on the edge, and you never know if they're going to dart across the road, or have sense to turn back around onto the prairie. They're just there frozen and you never know what choice they're going to make."

"It's *Waiting for Godot* on the Prairie. No, wait, *Little Dog on the Prairie*." I laughed again.

"No, Lucky, I am serious. It's like you are so paralyzed to make any choice, you make none. Run across the road if you need to, you may not get hit."

I could tell she had thought about the metaphor for awhile.

"Well, I like to think of myself more like a snow fence. Seemingly useless, a fence going nowhere."

Asha's face softened. "But if there's a horrible storm, I guess they come in handy."

Later in the day, I played a game. It was called insert Western metaphor into life:

I AM A _____.

TUMBLEWEED

LONE RANGER

HAWK

COW (EASILY HERDED)

COWBOY (ALONE)

SHEEPHERDER (EVEN BETTER)

MOUNTAIN RANGE

MEADOWLARK

WIND TURBINE

PUMPING JACK

REFINERY FLARE

OIL DERRICK

Somehow the game made me feel better, as I realized I was part of the Western way. Alone! Alone!

When my mother was first diagnosed with cancer, we went to an "Understanding Cancer" session. It was with a nurse with a round face in pink patterned scrubs with teddy bears on them. She handed us a stack of brochures all about cancer. All about chemo. What to expect when you weren't expecting. The last book in the packet was full of wigs and hats. My father was not with us, since we only had major medical insurance with a $35,000 deductible as he was a self-employed geologist, he was forced to work.

My mom and I took turns laughing at all the choices.

"I am going blonde!" She hooted.

"No, no, mom — it's all about this one." I pointed to a long redheaded mop.

When we got to the hats section, we noticed the turbans. There were two pages of them. Soft, T-shirt material turbans. In all the colors of the rainbow. Some of them looked like a bath towel on your head, others like silent film stars of the twenties.

"I want a turban."

It was after the black turban came and her hair did indeed all fall out that my mother became Indian in a way I had never known.

When people asked what kind of cancer my mother had, I lied. I said cervical, or ovarian, as it just seemed easier. When I said vaginal, people didn't know what to say. They don't want to hear it. Because it was more than having cancer, it was a taking away of something. Something more than a breast.

You want to know about vaginal cancer? It was like that damn prairie dog at the side of the road. You didn't know if it was going to run, to spread into every part of you, or if it was going to stay, retreat into where it came from. And the only thing I wanted to do was run over it. To crush it to bits. But of course, I couldn't do that. I drove her to treatment, and as she stopped eating, I learned to make Indian food, as it was the only thing she would eat: curd rice, rasam and rice, plain idlis, small dosas. For the first time, while she was propped up in a chair at the table, she explained how to use asafetida, how to use curry leaves when tempering spices, and how important it was to brown the onions with any curry.

On the day she tried to teach me how to brown mustard seed, cumin, and urad dal, I kept burning them. The mustard seed would crack and the lentils turned black.

"Slowly, slowly," my mother moved her hand to show how I should take it from the heat and roll the pan from side to side.

"I'll never learn all this," I said.

"Lakshmi, ma, I only need one dish," was her reply. "Just do one thing well."

After days of playing cowboys, Asha was ready to play Indian.

I hadn't known the rehearsal dinner was going to be Indian food until I saw the flier for *A Passage to India* catering in Denver. We had no Indian restaurants in Casper. The only one in the state was in Laramie, and that was recent.

The dinner was going to be in our house. Asha had long given up the idea of having a tent, and instead the reception was at the local Elks Hall. My father was a member.

All day, our house was full of Indians. They were a team of five. And although they drove down with most of the food cooked, I watched as they moved around the kitchen.

One of them, a young man who couldn't have been much over twenty, was setting up the steam trays. He had a head of thick black hair and a thin moustache. His nametag read SULTANA.

"What are you making?"

"Ma'm. We are making what Ms. Asha suggested. Rice, naan, chicken vindaloo, saag paneer, dal. And gulab jamuns." He seemed pleased at the menu. They also had brought maroon tablecloths and were turning our house into a mini India. A fat Ganesha was on every table.

"It smells good," I replied. And I left him to adjusting the Sterno.

Right after my mother died, my aunts came to stay for awhile. Not her sisters. My dad's sisters. As one of my mom's sisters was dead, and the other lived in Australia. It was too far to come. My Aunt Ivy and Aunt Lorraine both traveled from Iowa to help us out.

The first morning, I came into the kitchen and saw my Aunt Lorraine standing with the kitchen cupboard open. She was looking at the rows of jars and spices lined up. She picked one up, and then put it back.

"Oh, Lucky. I didn't see you. I was just looking at all this. Do you want me to keep this?" Lorraine had been emptying all the Western clothes out of my mom's closet. All her saris still made a riot of color in the top shelves of her closet.

"No, keep it. I've been cooking since she's been sick. And my dad likes it, so I guess I'll keep cooking."

"Nathan always did like spicy food," she said. "So I'll leave this."

Which was true. My dad could eat hotter food than I. And he loved Indian food. When my mom was alive, we ate it most nights. Nathaniel Thompson may have been raised on an Iowa farm, but he liked my mom's cooking. He loved my mother in a sari. He loved that she had decorated our house with embroidered wall hangings and carpets from Jaipur. My parents were the best couple I knew.

Hours before the rehearsal dinner was to start, Asha asked me to help her put on a sari. I was also to dress all her bridesmaids, who were all white. There were seven of them. All from the East, except one girl who was from California. Only one of them had ever been to Wyoming. And she had been to Jackson on a ski trip.

"It's pretty different here," she said.

I didn't say much. A refinery greeted you on one end of town, a Super Wal-Mart on the other. The other refinery had been closed for environmental reasons years ago, and the city had built over it with a golf course. Golfers played under a green of oil spills. Yes, it was different. I think Jackson even had a building code that everything had to be built in a log cabin style. To make people feel like they were in a real Western kind of place. Even their Kmart was a log cabin. Because god forbid you came on your vacation and saw an ugly strip mall. That would be no vacation at all. That would be too much real life. And what we wanted most of the time was a façade, a shell that covered up all the shit that was inside.
I told the girls to line up in sari blouses and skirts, and then one by one, I began to dress them.

When my mother was getting really bad, she spent most days in bed. She listened to a CD of ragas. She looked at photos. When she was awake, she told me funny India stories, about being on her grandfather's farm. I had never been to India; it was something we always planned but didn't ever do. We once had gone to Australia to visit her sister. But mostly my mom just slept.

I made her curd rice and tried to feed her at lunchtime. But in the end, I just brought her a protein shake and barked at her to drink it. I was tired. And I wanted her to eat. I helped her to the bathroom, and when she didn't make it, I cleaned up after her, and washed her.

About a week before she went into the hospital, she asked me about the funeral.

It wasn't at that point a hard thing to talk about. We had decided on the flowers, the readings, and the music. She even had chosen a photo of herself for the program. It was taken soon after we had moved to Wyoming. She was in sari and a down coat. She was in the backyard after the first snow of the year, and she was laughing. What always made us laugh about the picture was her hair. It was thick and almost down to her ankles. It was a beautiful photo.

"Lucky. I have to ask you something. I want you to promise something," she said.

"Okay. I promise." I felt at that point not promising anything to someone who was dying was just cruel.

"Lucky. I can't be buried in Western clothes. I had a dream last night that I was in my coffin, and you were burying me in a frilly pink nightgown. Promise me I won't be in Western clothes."

This was an easy promise. "Of course," I said.

"No Lucky, not a salawaar. In a sari. Those people in the funeral home won't know how." This was true. One night my mother had been rushed to the hospital with heavy bleeding. I was made to wait outside. But after about ten minutes a nurse came out and asked me if I could come unwrap my mother. Like she was a mummy. Like she was a gift.

My mother knew as well as I did that I didn't know how to put one on. In the few times we had Indian functions, she always dressed me. Here we hardly knew any other Indians. There was no occasion to learn.

My mother sat up in bed. "I want you to practice. You have to practice on me." She instructed me to her closet, where all her saris stacked up on each other like books.

"I want the green and gold one," she called out. And I

pulled out a green silk sari with a gold border and pallu. I chose a choli that matched and a slip.

My mother made sure I had picked the right things, and then I pulled off her nightgown. Her stomach was marked with blue X's for the radiation. Her skin was ashy, and there were tape marks on her skin where ivs and ports had been. I put her arms into the blouse, and carefully hooked the small clasps. Lying down, I slipped her slip over her legs and tied it tight at her waist. And then I carefully helped her stand up.

She walked me through every step. From the pleating to how to adjust the pallu. She made me put it on her twice, and then she asked me to dress myself. I stripped down and put on her same slip and blouse. But I chose another sari from the closet. It was also green, but dark green. It was a tie-dye, and there were white circles all over it. I put it on and turned to my mother.

"Okay?"

"You should wear saris more often. They're beautiful. You look so different. So beautiful…"

I looked at myself and thought I would like to wear them more often. But where? To the Wonder Bar? To work? Church was about the only place it might fly.

I took off the sari and my mother showed me the art of folding a sari. I put them back into the closet. And the whole time, I thought liar! Liar! Because I knew that if my mother died, I couldn't put her in a sari. Not because I didn't now know how. But it was different to dress someone lying down. Different to dress a stiff corpse. Different to dress your mother. Different to know that I was dressing someone for cremation. And I knew I couldn't do it. And in the end, she was cremated in a salwaar, but the green sari was wrapped around her like a shawl.

And now a bridesmaid from California wore the sari that I had worn that day with my mother. When I was done, the whole lot of them looked beautiful. They didn't wear them particularly well, but after a week of bandanas and jeans, they did look like a flock of parrots sitting in the upstairs bedroom. When they made their grand entrance downstairs, I could see my father's eyes look at the saris, and then at me. I was the only member of the bridal party not wearing one. Instead I wore a kurta top and jeans.

As the speeches began, I went out the back door. The house was hot and smelled like curry. Outside the wind bellowed. I stood on the lawn and listened to the air move through the cottonwoods. I picked up a cottonwood branch and broke it at a joint. Inside was a perfect star. Few people knew this.

"Were you liking the food?" A voice called out.

I turned and saw the same boy from before, Sultana. He was smoking a cigarette, which he dropped to the ground.

"Yes," I lied. I hadn't eaten anything, but instead had drunk glass after glass of champagne.

He pulled a maroon napkin from his pocket. He held a corner and let the wind blow it.

"The wind. I hear it all the time. Moving. I just want it to stop." He sighed.

"It's never still here." Then added, "You must miss home."

Sultana looked out into the party, and then back out onto the darkened lawn. "I'm from Goa. Have you been? The most beautiful beaches…"

"I've never been to India."

He didn't register any surprise. "You should go. Beautiful beaches."

I held out the cottonwood branch and moved it so it caught the light. "You see this? There is a perfect star inside." I handed him the branch, and he looked at it.

"It's magic," I said. When I was little, I thought they were fairy wands.

"Magic," he repeated.

"I'm sure this wasn't what you were expecting," I said. And I wasn't sure if I meant the party, Wyoming, Colorado, America for that matter, or even me.

"Why would anyone choose to live here?" He snapped the branch into smaller pieces.

And all I could say back was another question, "Why would anyone choose to leave their home, what they know?" I expected him to say the immigrant cliché — for something better, a new life, for more money, the experience. But instead he put the small branch into his pocket and held my gaze.

"Alan Ladd. *Shane*. It was a good movie, no? Magic." He pointed his fingers at me like mock guns, and with that, was called back into the house.

The day she died, she had been awake and irritable all day, and found me full of questions. I couldn't figure out what she wanted. I brought her a cup of tea, which she said no to. I tried to rub lotion on her hands, and she barked at me. I asked her if she wanted another pillow, for me to read to her.

"Stop asking me questions!" She looked at me so intently. So I stopped. I sat by her bed, and wandered around the hospital halls in circular laps. I didn't know she would die later that day, but I knew the end was coming. I wanted her in those last moments to tell me something profound, something that would change my life. I wanted her to be my compass — to tell me where to go.

And what I wanted the most was for her to tell me to get the hell out of Wyoming. To go to India. To live a different life. But instead, before she slipped off into a coma and her breathing became slow and almost nonexistent, she told me one thing.

"Take care of your father," she said this slowly, her eyes opening and closing.

And when you came right down to it, it was the most Indian thing she could say. Staying was the most Indian thing I could do.

When the party ended, I helped clean up. Sultana slipped in and out of the house filling the van from the restaurant. I wondered if he liked Asha's father-in-law-to-be's Stetson, which he had scarcely taken off in a few days. We didn't talk again. I was tired from the week of dress-up. Of playing cowboy one day, Indian the next. It was like Halloween. People are always so insanely happy to try something on. Especially when it is exotic. And since her guests were all from New York, and used to seeing Indians, I hadn't counted on Wyoming being the more exotic of the two. Now all we needed was to find a shaman to perform the wedding, and the trifecta would be complete.

Right after she died, while my dad and I sat by her beside, still not completely sure she was gone, her nurse came in to check. "She's gone," she said. And then she cracked open the window. It was cold and windy as hell that day, but her nurse was Native American, Arapahoe I thought. She looked at us and said, "It's to let the spirit out." But sitting there in the hospital room, I only felt the cold. And the wind felt the same as ever, screaming and shrill. I felt the chill not of death, but the fact that India was gone as well. I loved my father fiercely, but he didn't know what it was like to be brown.

Someone told me that grief is only being able to see what's been taken away from you. That I should look at all that I was given. But for me grief hung like those snow fences, exposed and present, even when it wasn't snowing. All I could see was what I would never understand, all that I would never know.

I hadn't really known that many Native Americans, but since I was biracial, I had been asked from time to time what tribe I was from. There were mostly Arapahoe and Shoshone, but as you moved northeast in Wyoming, there were Crow. And South Dakota near the Black Hills was full of Sioux. For the most part, I didn't mind being mistaken.

But once, when I was in college, my parents came to drive me home at the end of the year. I went to school in Minnesota, and we spent a day driving across South Dakota, stopping in a small town late at night. My father went in to get a motel room while my mom and I waited in the car.

He came out smiling and told us the room number.

"Room 202. Go through the lobby and up the stairs. I'll bring the bags up."

So, empty handed, my mom and I headed to the room. We weren't five feet from the stairs when we heard a scolding voice.

"Stop! Stop! You girls can't go up there!" the hotel worker, who was an older white lady, yelled to us.

I froze, but my mother smiled sweetly. "My husband just checked in, he's bringing in the bags, and we're going up to the room," she said.

I could tell that old hag was trying to compute. Trying to match us to my father. And as if a light clicked on, she smiled, "Oh, sorry girls! I thought you were heading to the third floor. It's full of hunters. I thought you were visiting from the reservation." She looked at us. "But you ain't that kind of Indian, are you?"

"No," was my mother's reply.

When we got upstairs, I refused to unpack. "She thought we were whores!" And I began to cry. My mother held me close and we said nothing to my father. But we never stayed at that chain again. My mother made sure of it.

When people asked me about being biracial, I had a pat answer. "It's the best of two worlds! I get to be American, and Indian. I have two cultures to choose from!" But everyone knows you tend to be more like one world. And mine was Wyoming. I was just brown, so that made it harder. I hated the half worlds inside me, because that's what made me paralyzed, and that's why I now sat not joining around the fire pit in the yard, while in saris, they all made s'mores and drank beer. All the halves did not make my whole.

The morning of the wedding, I woke late. I didn't put on coffee. Instead, I took the urn full of my mother's ashes and went to my truck. We drove around a bit, and I told her all about the wedding so far. I felt like a lunatic. And then I began to drive up the mountain. The wedding was in a little more than an hour. I knew I was missing the bridesmaid photos, but I navigated up the mountain road. I drove up East End Road to Crimson Dawn, to my special spot. Right after my mother died, I had brought a handful of her ashes and spread it off the back side of the mountain. From Crimson Dawn, you could see the Ferris Mountains and the Big Horns. I sat focusing out at Muddy Mountain. But there was nothing transformative there. There was the just the wind and the smell of Ponderosas. I wanted some sort of secret to be told to me. I thought that it wasn't that Asha was marrying white. It wasn't even that she had called me a prairie dog. And maybe this wasn't about my mother at all. It was that I hated how the West, this place, had been reduced to a movie set or a backdrop for a story that had nothing to do with here. It was a kind of screensaver. And India was the same way. It was the saris, a little dancing, some food the caterers had cooked. It wasn't real. I didn't know how you really knew a place at all. We were always dressing up into different personas; everything was always being presented in a choreographed way, from vacations to eating out. Even poor Sultana had been made to wear a tuxedo with a turban. Maybe I needed to watch more movies for the answers. I didn't know what was real.

I knew that if I sat much longer, I would be late. And although they didn't need me to dress them, I needed to get down and put the pink silk bridesmaid dress on. I needed to play the part of the doting sister.

I drove down the dirt road back towards the main mountain road. Little clouds of earth whirled at the wheels. A fine dirt coated my windshield. It was then that I saw the prairie dog, poised like a mirage emerging from the smoke. I didn't even have time to make a knowing eye contact with the creature, because that's how things really happen, so fast that you thrive on instinct.

Would it change anything to tell you I missed? That the animal ran to the edge of the road and disappeared into the tall grass? Or would it change it all to tell you that I went to the wedding, still hearing the bones crack beneath the weight of the wheels, still feeling the speed of my own escape.

Reserve Champion

I t was the eye of the deer that Delia saw first. A cold black button that was a fixed mark, looking into her sewing room window. Delia sat down in front of her Bernina and looked out the frame. Her neighbor, Chip Boe, had come back from hunting all right. And what a scraggly deer! Its coat was mangy looking, the rack broken. Chip must have come home in the night. Where was his license for? Up near the Big Horns? The Absarokas? Delia had forgotten. His wife, Carol Boe, had prattled on, cigarette in hand, about how she and her daughter Margaret were going to have girl time while Chip was hunting.

"Mags and I are going to watch movies and do facials," Carol had said over the fence. "Aren't we, Mags?"

Margaret was five and probably didn't even know what a facial was. Her nose was running and she looked over at her mother from the seat of her three-wheeler. She continued to circle the patio with her trike. Her too-big pink helmet fell over her eyes. Her blonde hair was matted.

"It must be a regular girl's night for you and Ivory over there," Carol said looking over to where Delia's daughter was playing.

"Yeah, well, with Ivory's rehearsals and all, we get to bed early," Delia said. "The weather sure is turning."

"Yep. It's getting cold all right. Poor Mags. She loves that bike, and come the snow, she's only got this patio here to ride on. I keep telling her she's gonna wear a rut in the concrete." Carol laughed her smoker's laugh and lit up another cigarette. "It better stay warm enough for Chip to bring home the bacon. If it snows, he'll just sit in a cabin with his buddies drinking beer."

Now looking at the gutted deer, she thought Chip had brought home the bacon, but why had he hung it there? The Boe's yard had a few straggly cottonwoods which in the summer blew a fine down into Delia's yard. But Chip had hoisted the deer from the rafters over their covered patio, right above the track where Margaret rode her bike. The carcass dangled miserably close to Delia's window. The deer hung by its back legs, its flanks spread wide. Was it a mule deer? It must be. They were in season. It was mid-October and already the ground was frozen.

The deer's eyes were wide open. From its mouth, Delia could see a wedge of pink tongue. Delia's eyes moved down to her machine. She began work on an embroidered piece of trim. She was sewing a kind of lederhosen for a doll. For a Dress-Doll-Competition. Her hands shook as she moved the foot of the machine down onto the fabric. The eye watched her. There were no drapes to close across the window. Delia needed the hard prairie light to sew.

When Ivory came home from school in the afternoon, she regarded the deer through the window. She chewed on an apple and looked to Delia.

"Why are they hanging it there? Ain't they going to eat it?'

"Don't say ain't. They're going to eat it all right. Chip's

just waiting to butcher. He's tenderizing the meat. It's freezing outside. It'll be okay. Don't look at it."

"You can see its tongue. Look, Mama, it's sticking out its tongue at you."

"No, it isn't. It's frozen that way. It's sticking out its tongue at Chip and Carol."

Ivory and Delia watched through the fence as Margaret came outside. Her winter coat was wide open. On her feet were church shoes, black patent leather ones. Her nose was running and she held her hand up to mouth and coughed. Margaret had a chronic cough. She got onto her bike and began to circle the patio. Ignoring the deer, she looped and looped under the carcass.

"Ivory, you go practice the piano now. You got lessons at four. Then swimming after that. Pack your suit. We don't have time to come home in between. You need a protein shake to tide you over?"

"Nah." She headed to the piano. "You think Katelynn will like the new piece?" Ivory was ten and had played the piano since she was four. Her long brown hair hung down her thin back. Delia put her hair in curlers every night so each end hung like a helix next to Ivory's bright face.

"She'll love it." Delia's stomach turned and she looked down at her shaking hands. She went into her sewing room and closed the door. She looked around the room. Against the window was her machine. She rested her hands against a large table she used to cut patterns; stacks of fabrics sat folded like books on the edge of the table. Next to the table was her trophy case. It was stuffed with ribbons from the county and state fairs, contests and competitions — all from her handiwork. *Reserve Champion. Reserve Champion. Reserve Champion.* The pale pink rosettes made a garden in her case. Reserve Champion. It was better than first place all right, but not quite the best. It was a kind of purgatory of ribbons. People understood champion, they even understood first place. But Reserve Champion? All Delia could say was it was like First Runner Up in a beauty contest. Only it wasn't — the Reserve Champion went on to the state fair as well. Just under slightly lower expectations. Only one trophy lay in the case. An ornate cup with a flat gold square pronouncing her achievement. *Delia Chalk, The Lazarus Award, Natrona County High School, 30th Class Reunion.* The Lazarus award. Last spring, plain as day, her reunion newsletter had come. And there she was, listed as dead in the newsletter. Deceased, forty-nine, Chalk, Delia (Coffey). *Deceased.* She wasn't dead. She called the school and her old class president, Joe Weeks. I am not dead, she kept saying to herself. *I am Delia Chalk. I have two girls. Katelynn and Ivory. I make clothes. My girls are talented. One's going to be a country star, the other can do anything — play the piano, tap dance, swim, paint, sew, ice skate* (her head spun when she thought of all of the classes she drove Ivory to). *I am not dead.*

She had gone to the reunion in a green silk suit that had taken her two weeks to sew. Her frame was heavyset and she cut the skirt on the bias so as to look slimmer. She dyed her hair a toasted chestnut and dug through small bullet-shaped white lipsticks samples from Avon till she found one that made her lips look like cherries. When she checked in, Marla Stamps, who was now Marla Weeks, looked at Delia with surprise.

"Delia, we thought you were dead."

"No, didn't Joe tell you? I am alive and well. I even had another child since the last reunion! Ivory's ten. My Katelynn's almost twenty-five. She lives in Nashville now. Trying to make it in the music industry." Delia combed through her purse for pictures of the girls. Marla smiled.

"Sounds good. Say, you're going to have to make a nametag. We thought you were dead. All the rest here are printed." Marla pointed a neat row of printed tags.

Delia wrote her name in big block letters with a black marker. DELIA CHALK. Then she worried that people wouldn't know who she was, so she took another tag. DELIA COFFEY CHALK. Her husband Walt Chalk had been dead for almost eleven years. Killed by a heart attack. He was chopping their winter firewood and had died in the forest. A man died in a forest and no one was there to hear him.

The reunion was a wash and a full weekend to boot. Delia moved from group to group. All of them regarded her warmly. She was Delia. She was never class president, but secretary. Not prom queen, but she had been in charge of the decorations. She wasn't unpopular, she had always been invited to things. Delia had been at parties. Gone to the dances. She had even made dresses for other girls in her class. But she wasn't who people remembered when they thought back to high school. Marla was. *Reserve Champion.* Even Marla's senior prom dress had been the deep purple of a champion ribbon.

Delia had stayed in Casper all her life. Through boom and bust. She prided herself on living in the city and raising Ivory where there was culture. In Casper, there was community theatre, a mall (the largest in Wyoming), a community college, and the symphony. She was born out near Alcova and spent her first school years in a one-room schoolhouse. She had gotten her hardship license when she was fifteen and drove the hour into Casper every morning, determined to go to a real high school. But, at times, Casper seemed, well, so small to her. When in fact, for a small town, it spread wide across the prairie. From the lookout point on the mountain, Casper looked like a large black stain against the taupe plain.

It was at the awards ceremony the final night when Joe called Delia up to the podium.

"And this year's Lazarus Award goes to Delia Coffey. Delia Coffey Chalk. We all thought she was dead. But it turns out she is alive and well. Why don't you tell us what you've been doing, Delia?"

Delia smoothed down the taffeta dress she was wearing for the last night's banquet. The black fabric had a pattern of swirls that looked like fingerprints. She moved to the podium and gripped the trophy. It was heavy. Looking at her was her remaining class. Their eyes fixed upon her. Delia's mouth felt dry. Stop staring, she thought. Her hands shook.

"Well, I am indeed alive. I have two girls. One of them is going to be a country star...the other's still in elementary school. Actually, I think we should spend a minute of silence for those in our class who have truly died. Pete Sims. Maewille Schwandt." Delia bowed her head. Her classmates looked down to their banquet tables laden with tough chicken and sweating iced tea glasses. Delia was glad she had made them uncomfortable. She racked her brain for other dead class members. "I think we should all just thank the Lord that we are all here and alive. These thirty years sure have flown." Delia moved down from the stage clutching the shiny cup. She would show them she was alive all right.

Yet now, leaning against the sewing table, she felt sick. She looked out the window. It was that the deer didn't blink. Its cold look didn't move. Snow fell down from the sky and Delia saw that that was why Chip had hung the deer from the patio. He didn't want to deal with snow. The doll she was dressing lay on the table. Her head was full of golden curls, her lips lightly parted, eyes closed. Her eyes opened when you moved her from lying down to sitting up. *Fräulein Gretchen,* thought Delia. She was making a whole German outfit for her. Right down to the petticoats. She had even knit little socks. When The National Bank of Wyoming had announced the competition weeks ago, Delia knew she would win. The contest was to dress a doll in some sort of international outfit. Walt years ago had been stationed in Germany. She'd seen enough to know that this contest was in the bag. Who else would win? Three weeks ago they'd all gone to the bank to pick up their dolls, and she saw her competition. She knew Patti Combers' sewing. Sloppy. Jen Ruiz. Good, but she didn't have the time Delia did. The bank manager handed each lady a doll.

"Here you go." The manager had handed Delia a black doll.

"This is nice. But I think I need a white doll. One of those." She pointed to Patti and Jen who were clutching dolls the color of putty.

"Well, hmmm. Are you sure you put that on your registration?"

Delia smiled. "I fill out registration forms all the time. I am regular at this sort of thing. I know I specified white."

"Well, perhaps you can trade with Mrs. Gupta there. I think she wanted a darker doll." The manager pointed at a small brown woman who was skulking at the back of the room. "She's the new doctor's wife. From IN-DIA," she said slowly.

Delia turned the doll over in her hands. Its mechanism was broken; its wide eyes remained open. There was no way Delia was keeping this doll. Delia approached Mrs. Gupta, who held in her arms a naked white doll.

"Ms. Oates here says you might be interested in a trade?" Delia held out the black doll to the woman. Mrs. Gupta looked deep at Delia, her black eyes rimmed in kohl. She took the doll and handed Delia her own. Delia wondered if she could even speak English. She brought Gretchen home and began work. She had even fashioned a hat with a small feather in it.

Delia picked Gretchen up. Her eyes opened. The deer looked in from outside.

"Ivory!" Delia called. She couldn't sew now. "Get your

things. We're leaving early. I'm just gonna go talk to the Boes first." Delia gathered her purse and headed next door.

Margaret answered the door. The smell of smoke and heat moved onto Delia.

"Your mama here?"

Margaret nodded and closed the front door, leaving Delia on the stoop. Good God, thought Delia. Carol is such a bad mother. The smoking. She didn't cook. She saw how often the Schwann's truck stopped at the door. They often had loud parties and had a fire pit in their yard. When they had first moved in more than ten years ago, they were a newly married couple. Delia had brought over food, offered to help Carol wallpaper. Now look at them. Margaret was always in a mish-mash of clothes, boys' clothes, that Carol's sister had given her.

"Hey there, Delia. What's up?" Carol said as she opened the door.

"It's the deer. I see Chip's done all right."

"Yeah, well, you know usually Chip takes it right in for processing. But it's so cold and all. He thought he might do it himself this year. His brother Abe's coming down from Afton to help. But he can't come til the weekend. Maybe Sunday. You and Ivory want some meat?"

"No. I don't like game." Delia looked to Ivory, who sat in the idling car, reading a book. It was Tuesday. "Listen, it makes Ivory nervous. She feels bad. You know, cartoons and all," Delia lied.

"Sorry, Delia. We'll butcher as soon as we can. Mags here hardly even notices it. She thinks it's a new pet." Carol looked past Delia to the car. "You tell Ivory that when Chip hunts, he's real humane. One shot, maybe two. You sure I can't send over some deer steaks? You like antelope? I think Abe might bring us some antelope."

"Yeah, well, no. We don't eat game." A bitter taste rose in her throat as Delia went to the car. Delia thought about her own father, who hunted antelope every season. Delia had hated the taste of the meat. It was so sagey. You could tell the antelope had a diet of sagebrush. Her mother would make chili with the meat, trying to mask the taste of sage and the antelope's adrenaline with tomatoes and kidney beans. But that taste of the prairie was in every bite. Delia felt herself start to gag. She spat into the snow.

By the second day, the deer's eyes had started to cloud to an opaque shade, almost like a blind man. Delia hung a piece of fabric over the window and brought in a halogen lamp from the music room to sew to. Her spirits were lifted. Today she would take the doll to the bank; by tomorrow the Champion ribbon would be hers. Right after her class reunion had been the county fair, which Delia had entered. Technically, Ivory had entered, but Delia made the outfit. She sewed a suit — all out of wool that was Wyoming raised (she had liked that touch). Ivory complained that no ten-year-olds wore suits. But Delia held firm. It was tasteful. Delia oversaw all the sewing projects for Ivory's 4-H group, and in her group (The Baker's Dozen) none of the girls were going to wear anything disrespectful. Suits, skirt and culottes. All respectable separates. When the prizes were announced, Delia was crushed. Ivory only got a first place ribbon. Although the sewing was good, Ivory flubbed in the interview as to how she made it, and even worse, had not done well in the fashion show. All the kids were made to model their outfits, and Ivory walked down the runway in a straight line, not smiling, looking miserable. Delia even got her a leather briefcase. She swung it like a machete. It was no wonder. Yes, August was a terrible month. But the bank was a chance in the winter to gain something back. Delia looked at Gretchen. *Fräulein Gretchen.*

She began ripping out the seams of Gretchen's vest. On her sewing table were the cut-out pieces of Ivory's new skating dress. If only Ivory were better at things. She's not at all like Katelynn, thought Delia. Katelynn was natural when it came to everything. Singing. Dancing. She was singing the national anthem at rodeos and monster truck shows before she was Ivory's age. She'd now been in Nashville two years. She sang at bars and who knows where else.

The threads unraveled with ease. Delia squinted at the tiny stitches. She thought again of Katelynn. She closed her eyes.

Two weeks ago Ivory had called into her sewing room. "Mama!"

"Yes, baby?"

"Mama, Katelynn's on the phone. She says she's got news." Delia's heart had pounded. Katelynn. Could this be it? She picked up her extension.

"Hey, Mama," Katelynn's voice echoed over the line. "Guess what, Mama — I'm getting married."

"Married. To who? When?" Her hands had begun to shake. A bitter taste filled her mouth.

"Can I come to the wedding? Can I be a flower girl?" Ivory chimed in from the kitchen phone.

"Yes, of course you can, Ive. Mama, what do you mean, to whom — to Jerry. You remember Jerry. You met him. Jerry from the insurance office. And we're not getting married right away. We haven't set a date. We're gonna wait, 'cause I want to look good in my wedding pictures. And you can't look good pregnant," Katelynn laughed into the phone.

Thinking now about her laugh, the lightness in her voice, the same sourness came up her throat. Delia spat on the floor and gripped the ripper. The piece of calico covering the window slipped down. The deer spun a little in the wind. Its eyes moved back and forth like it was nodding at her.

Delia had called for Ivory to hang up the phone. Ivory had groaned and the kitchen extension had clicked.

"You're pregnant? Katelynn. Why? What about your career?"

"I can still have a career. Mama, I am having twins. Boys. Due in March. You're gonna be a grandma."

"I already am a grandma. Or did you forget that?"

"No I didn't." Katelynn's voice grew cold and clipped. "Look, Mama, I thought you'd be happy for me. I got to go. I got to get back to work." The phone clicked dead.

"No. Katelynn. I am sorry. Of course I'm happy. Twins? Are there any other country stars with twins? You could write lullabies," Delia had spoken to the dial tone.

Ivory slinked in out of nowhere and had stood in the doorframe. "Mama, are we going to the wedding? Will she get married in Nashville or here? Can I sing at the wedding? Am I going to be an aunt?"

"I don't know anything, Baby. Your sister's got a mind of her own," Delia had replied. "You go now. Read. Go play with Margaret. Just go." Ivory disappeared into the mouth of the house. Delia had sat with the phone in her lap for the next two hours.

And now Delia opened her eyes. She ripped and began sewing again with quick strokes. She had to take Gretchen to the bank. Delia picked the doll up. Her eyes looked at Delia, looked outside. The deer continued to nod. No, it seemed to say. Shame on you, its shaking head implied.

By the evening, Gretchen was propped up at the bank next to teller station three. The bank was one of the few buildings downtown that seemed full of activity; the rest of the downtown had a deflated air that began when the mall opened on the east side of town in the eighties. The atmosphere inside the bank was one of modern efficiency. A popcorn machine greeted customers in the foyer, inside were tables full of brochures on everything from financing a college education to opening an IRA. The bank was all blues and white; it gave Delia the feeling of being at sea. The tellers' high desks formed a horseshoe around the floor. Delia thought Gretchen's location was quite central. She had been the first to bring her doll into the bank. Patti and Jen had also brought their dolls soon after — a Hawaiian doll and English one. Both were weak compared to Gretchen. Patti looked at Delia's doll and laughed.

"Delia. It looks like it's snowing in the south on that doll."

Delia laughed. "Her petticoats are supposed to show. Look. I used the serger to scallop the edge." She lifted Gretchen's skirt. But already Patti had turned away and was talking to Jen. The results would be posted tomorrow by noon. On Friday would be an awards ceremony in which the winner would not only get a prize but a hundred-dollar savings bond. Delia thought she'd give the bond to Ivory, but now wondered if she should start a savings account for the new babies. Would Katelynn like that? Her head catalogued the fabric she kept in the basement. She could make christening outfits for both of them. Sailor suits. Real suits. She grew excited thinking about the possibilities.

The snow that had begun yesterday had tapered off. Corn snow. The flakes were big and icy. Delia set the dinner table and lit candles. She always cooked dinner and insisted that she and Ivory use cloth napkins and eat like ladies. Ivory put down the forks and put a spoon above the plates for dessert. Delia and Ivory ate every meal off fine bone china.

"Mama, you know at the fair, they have a table decorating category. You can set the table up real fancy."

"I know. Maybe next year you can do that. I don't think we should do sewing. You want to make jam? Though it might be too late to get crabapples... We should think about getting some sort of animal. A bunny? Maybe we could keep a chicken."

Ivory looked out the dining room window.

"Look. Margaret's hitting that deer."

Delia looked out the window and squinted. It was already dark, but floodlights lit up the patio. Margaret held in her hands a large cottonwood branch. She was hitting the deer again and again. The frozen body moved back and forth. Delia walked out through the back door and up to the fence.

"Margaret. Why you hitting that thing? Stop it."

Margaret stopped and looked at Delia. "It's my piñata." Her stick poked into the flanks. Ivory ran up behind Delia.

"It ain't no piñata. You keep hitting it and guts and blood will come out," Ivory shouted.

Delia looked at the girls. "No blood will come out. It's frozen. It's just not humane. It's not nice, Margaret. It's not what a lady does." Close up, the deer's eyes were milky. Delia averted her eyes to the Boes' wrought iron picnic table, which was littered with ashtrays.

Carol came out the back door. Her blonde hair was in a messy ponytail. She wore a pink sweatsuit and was holding a cigarette.

"I was just telling Margaret here that it's not ladylike to hit an animal," Delia explained.

"Ah, Delia. It ain't going to hurt it. Look at that coat. We ain't keeping it. This poor guy looks like he had a hard life. I think Chip put him out of his misery!" Carol laughed.

The pitch in Delia's voice rose. "But it's not ladylike. Little ladies don't hit things." The deer rocked back and forth like a pendulum. The low chain link fence between them was cold to Delia's touch as she gripped it.

Carol's eyes squinted into Delia's dark yard. "I don't think you're one to talk about the ways little ladies work."

Delia let go of the fence. "It's cold," she mumbled. "Let's go eat, Ivory." She walked back into the house. From the outside, the dining table was illuminated by the candles. Delia turned back to Carol. "I've made stew tonight. You guys want some? Did you cook?"

"That'd be real nice, Delia."

Carol turned to go back inside. Margaret took another swing.

When Katelynn got pregnant, she was fourteen. Walt had just died and Delia was distracted. Walt, who had been older than Delia, was supposed to work for years more. Delia had never had a job, she'd never gone to college. Delia went to work at a fabric shop and began her sewing business on the side. They had some savings, and Delia was ready to be prudent. If only she had a son. Her own father was an old-fashioned man and was happy to leave her money, as long as she had a son.

Katelynn was wild that summer. She sang that national anthem regularly at little league games and went around singing at small rodeos and rodettos. She had a regular gig at the funeral home singing two hymns for fifty bucks a pop. Delia was happy Katelynn was earning her own money. Happy that her daughter had friends she could pal around with. And then by August she was three months pregnant. The father was a kid from Star Valley who was spending the summer in the big city of Casper, working for the park service and doing rodeo at night. He never knew he was a father.

For Delia, the decision to have the baby was never a question. The baby would be born. But Katelynn was still a child. Her life would be over with a new baby. Delia withdrew Katelynn from school and told the district she would home school. She arranged that the baby would be born in Denver. Katelynn was small and up until her seventh month didn't look that pregnant, as long as she wore baggy clothes. Well into that fall, she still saw her friends and no one knew. Instead Delia told everyone she herself was pregnant. Told them it was a miracle. That Walt had left her with this gift. She was a big woman, and with all her extra fat, no one questioned her. She told her father he'd now have a grandson. Her mother worried that Delia, who was nearing forty, was too old to be having a baby. Delia laughed and sewed. She hoped no one really did the math.

When Katelynn neared eight months, Delia kept her close to the house. She told her this was for her career. Katelynn didn't care. She watched satellite TV and talked on the phone, telling her friends she had mono. Delia drove Katelynn the two-hundred eighty miles to Denver for routine check-ups. Ivory Alice Chalk was born in Denver at the beginning of March. Delia told friends that she and Katelynn had gone down to Denver to shop and the baby just came. And that was that.

The National Bank of Wyoming dominated the downtown of Casper. It was a squat structure built in the 1960s. It was sandwiched between solid buildings built during the second World War. The masonry was brick and poking off the roof was an antennae-like clock that proclaimed the time and temperature. Delia maneuvered her van into a parking space outside and checked her reflection in the car mirror. Ivory sat sullenly eating a granola bar in the passenger seat. Delia left the car running and Ivory sulking. Entering the bank, her thick glasses fogged at the warmth. She stood blinded for a moment. Taking her glasses off, she waved them in front of her, her eyes scanning to Gretchen. Her gaze stopped at the doll. A pale pink ribbon hung from her raised arm. *Honorable Mention.* Delia looked at the other dolls — the same pink ribbon hung from all of them. At the center of the bank, on a table on its own, by the deposit slips, stood the winning doll. Delia approached it.

JASMINE, said the name beneath the doll. I AM FROM INDIA! A sign beneath the doll proclaimed. Mrs. Gupta had wrapped Jasmine in a toga. Her black curly hair had been oiled down and smoothed back. Fake white flowers crowned her head. Mrs. Gupta had painted a red dot in the middle of the black doll's forehead. A purple ribbon hung pinned to the silk. The fabric was bright red and was woven with gold thread. Small peacocks danced across Jasmine's shoulder. Delia lifted up the skirt. Jasmine was barefoot. Barefoot!

Ms. Oates sidled up next to Delia. "Isn't she beautiful? So exotic."

"She's barefoot," Delia replied.

"Oh, don't you know. In India, they don't wear shoes. They're too poor." Ms. Oates shook her head and pursed her lips as if she were saddened by this fact.

"But, I don't think she sewed anything." Delia began to touch the doll. Except for the little midriff top that Jasmine wore (belly exposed), there was no sewing.

"You didn't win." Ivory too sidled up to Delia. In her hand was the limp Honorable Mention ribbon from Gretchen's arm. "No, your mama didn't win this one. The Indian dolly did." Ms. Oates picked a piece of sugared granola oats off Ivory's coat and pointed at Jasmine.

"Delia, this wasn't a sewing competition. It was a dress-a-doll. You didn't have to sew anything. But I sure like what you brought in. Reminds me of *The Sound of Music*. You know, when they run in the fields, on top of the mountain. You should have put a little guitar in her hand and named her Maria. That would've been a hoot." Ms. Oates tidied a stack of errant deposit slips.

"Is there a second place?" Delia let go of Jasmine.

"Nah, just the one big one. But come to the bank tomorrow. We have some prizes for all of you."

"Yes, thank you." Delia looked at Gretchen, whose upraised hand made her seem as if she was saluting. She took the ribbon from Ivory's hand and put it over Gretchen's shoulder like a bag.

"You should have picked a better country. That wasn't such a good choice," said Ivory.

Bitterness filled her mouth. Delia gagged. She needed to go home.

Only the Boes ever knew that Katelynn was pregnant. Carol and Chip were newlyweds, they moved into the house next door in November. The house had been empty for almost a year, abandoned by an oilman's family who hadn't survived the bust. Carol was always coming over to ask Delia for things. Coffee. A hammer. Delia would always keep her in the living room, telling her that Katelynn had mono and was contagious. But one afternoon when Delia came back from the fabric store, clear as day, Katelynn and Carol sat at the kitchen table eating Christmas cookies and drinking Kool-Aid. Katelynn's tummy strained from under her small All-State choir T-shirt. "I see you've met Katelynn," said Delia, putting down a sack of groceries.

"Yeah. Katelynn and I were just talking about her hair. I don't know how she keeps it so long." Katelynn's hair had grown thick and glossy with the baby.

Katelynn looked down. Carol stood up and crumpled her napkin into a ball. "Well, I better be getting home. Chip'll be home soon."

Delia walked her to the door. "What are the odds? That we would both be pregnant? I only wish my husband was here to see this. The thing is," Delia paused. "We can't have two new babies. And Katelynn being so young and all. She's giving hers up for adoption. We're just not telling people this. Can you understand this?"

Carol looked at Delia in her quilted winter coat. On her lapel were a large poinsettia brooch and a smaller pin that proclaimed *Jesus is the Reason for the Season!*

"Yeah, sure. I understand. Must be tough, though, for you. To give up your own grandchild."

Delia's face fell. "It is."

And once Ivory was born, Katelynn seemed barely interested in the baby. She looked at her pink face and black eyes once Ivory was all wrapped up in a thin blanket then asked Delia to get her a Coke. When they came home, Delia herself began to feel as if she had given birth. Katelynn slid right back into life. By that summer, she was singing at rodeos again, but coming home by midnight. She told Delia as soon as she graduated from Natrona County High School, she would blow this popsicle stand. And that's exactly what she did. Delia helped her pack her car. Ivory clutched onto to Delia's leg and barely registered Katelynn's absence. She moved to Denver, then on to Nashville. Delia had been happy to see her go. She hated being in the same room with both of them. She was glad to have Ivory to herself. To try again.

That night Delia sat in her sewing room with the lights off. She began to cry. The scraps of Gretchen's dress sat in a neat pile on her table. She always did what was right. Wasn't she right about Ivory? And now Katelynn was getting married and having another family. What about her dreams? She was going to make it, Delia knew it. She stared at her trophy case. *Reserve Champion.* The snow and moon outside illuminated the room. The trophy winked at her. Her gaze moved out the window. In the light, the deer looked like a cameo against the Boes' house. A white silhouette against the onyx of night. Delia picked up a piece of Ivory's skating skirt and blew her nose.

The ceremony at the bank was scheduled for ten o'clock. Delia took out the green suit she had worn to the reunion. A small mustard stain was next to the row of buttons. She scrubbed at it. Delia glanced outside. The snow was all melted. The day was well above freezing. That deer's going to thaw, she thought. She went into her sewing room to take a better stare out the window. The deer was gone, only frayed ropes hung from the rafters. Guess somebody can't wait till Sunday to butcher, she thought. Delia dressed.

At the bank, the ceremony was running late. Mrs. Gupta was nowhere to be found. Ms. Oates had set up a table of cookies and punch. She had tried to add a festive air to the bank. Looping like udders in front of the teller stations was a twist of blue and white crepe paper. The heady scent of popcorn filled the air. Teller three kept an air freshener at her station. When Delia walked by Gretchen, she caught a whiff of something vaguely tropical. She suspected this might have given Jasmine the edge. The tellers looked bored. Delia made small talk with Patti and the other girls. Ivory stood at a tall desk, filling out deposit slips that she took from a large stack in front of her. Last week Delia told the school that Ivory had a doctor's appointment, as she wanted her there for the ceremony. Now Delia wished she had left her at home with a video.

"It is nice fabric on that Jasmine. But there's no real workmanship. No sewing. I don't think that should be allowed." Delia sipped at her punch.

Patti, dressed head to toe in a tight velour track suit, crinkled her nose. "Gosh, Delia. It's good that she won. She probably needed the money. India's very poor."

"Her husband's a doctor," she replied. Delia couldn't believe the sympathy!

Half an hour later, Mrs. Gupta came into the bank with her husband, who was a short man wearing a suit and looking stern. Mrs. Gupta was wearing her own version of Jasmine's toga, with a pilled cardigan on top. Delia noted she was wearing sandals with socks underneath. Ms. Oates spoke loudly to the group. The few people depositing their paychecks or waiting for a loan officer looked over with mild interest and then went back to their business.

"This year, it is my pleasure to award Meenu Gupta as the champion of the National Bank of Wyoming's Dress-A-Doll Competition. This year, as many of you know, we had an international theme. Mrs. Gupta's doll represents her native county of India, where her doll, Jasmine, is from." Ms. Oates paused on the word India as if she was turning it over in her mouth like candy. "The bank would like to award you this savings bond for $100 and this trophy."

A trophy! Delia's eyes traveled to the cup. It was big with a golden doll affixed to the top like a lone bride on a wedding cake. Delia wanted to scream at the injustice. She should have kept the black doll. Maybe done Africa. That was poorer than India. Wasn't it?

"Look Mama, that trophy's bigger than yours!" Ivory pinched Delia's side. She held a half-filled cup of red punch and a fist of deposit slips.

"Shh!" said Delia.

Mrs. Gupta took the trophy and began to speak. Her accent was British and she spoke English perfectly well. "Thank you, Ms. Oates. It is a pleasure to get this. My husband Dr. Gupta and I are always happy to share things from our native land to yours. Jasmine's sari is though not perhaps practical for Wyoming winters." She paused. "We'd like to donate this savings bond. To the Lion's Club. For the blind camp on Casper Mountain. Thank you." She moved away from Ms. Oates.

Sari? Delia was sorry. That this woman had basically gift-wrapped a doll and won.

"I want one of those dresses, Mama. Maybe I can sew something like that for the fair next year," said Ivory.

"There ain't no sewing in that," Delia replied.

"Maybe Katelynn can wear something like that when she gets married."

Delia took Ivory by the arm and headed for the door. In her other hand, she clutched her plastic bag of prizes. A bank Frisbee, a keychain, and a plastic coffee mug. She dropped them in the trash on her way out the door. Ivory shook off Delia's grip the moment they moved outside.

"You're hurting me." She rubbed her upper arm with exaggerated motions.

Delia thought she didn't begin to know what hurt was.

It was after lunch while Delia was cutting out the rest of the pattern for the ice skating dress that she saw Chip outside. He was on the lawn, knife in hand. The deer was skinned and the head cut off. The legs were cut off as well. The deer looked small and its flesh marbled against the browning lawn. Chip tied ropes to the leg stubs and tried to hang the deer from a low cottonwood branch. The pelt, which Chip had not cut carefully off the carcass, lay like scraps of fabric around the body. Delia felt sick. As sick as she had been when she was pregnant with Katelynn. When everything she ate tasted like fat and the smell of any meat made her vomit. Walt brought her cola and cold compresses. He told her she was beautiful. That she was his girl.

Delia thought about the doll again. The trophy. Of Katelynn and her new babies. Of being dead but really being alive. About the deer's eyes. She put down her scissors. She wasn't going to leave Gretchen in that bank one more minute. It was near closing time when Delia arrived at the bank. Some of the tellers had already left. It was beginning to get dark. Delia walked with purpose through the front door. She saw Gretchen's raised hand had been moved down to her side. She was standing on her honorable mention ribbon. The grey wool of her dress, the petticoats — she looked so dignified. She belonged there. Yet, there was something sneering in her expression, in her fixed face. Delia walked toward her and then turned past the row of a dozen or so dolls. She veered to the center table where Jasmine stood. Delia kept walking and grabbed Jasmine. She meant at first to just take the ribbon, but the silk felt cool to her touch. She tightened her grip and squeezed. She stuffed the doll into her coat.

The black bubble behind which the ceiling cameras rolled watched Delia. Fixed ebony blisters. The hard unblinking stare. Delia moved through the glass doors of the lobby out into the winter air. It was warming up, it was well above freezing. Delia ran and as she did, the doll fell from her grasp. Where had she parked? The silk unfurled like a flag from her shaking hands. The doll dropped nearly naked into the snow. Its bright, clear eyes closed.

Fenced Out

They were coming back from vacation when the accident happened. One moment Madhu was looking out the car window. *An antelope! A cow!* And then there was the *bump bump* of the car flipping over, the contents (them) being spread out onto the open road. She looked up at her arm and her crumpled fist. Her fingers were coated in sugar, she had been feeding the children rotis in the back seat. Miles back, eight-year-old Sameer had asked to stop at a restaurant for breakfast. He liked dispensing straws from their containers, eating food wrapped in waxed paper in which the grease pooled. But Vikram was in a hurry. Always in a hurry. They had been gone from the motel in Cheyenne for five days, and he feared his brother Anik would regret his decision to sponsor them if they went on this vacation. So instead they stopped at a McDonald's only to use the bathroom. As Madhu pulled five-year-old Kavita and twelve-year-old Priyanka from the car, Vikram and Sameer were already behind the fingerprinted glass doors. For a moment she wondered if they should forget money and eat there. But by the time she and the girls had used the toilet, Vikram was already back in the car, the engine running.

The scent of McDonald's stayed with them for a mile or so down the road. The grease and coffee smells made all of their stomachs turn. She twisted to dig behind the back seat and noticed Sameer had a pile of ketchup packets on his lap. In Kavita's was a mound of pink sweetener packs. She pulled out a Tupperware container and began to separate the rotis. She had made them two days ago in the kitchen (next to boxes of instant oatmeal and soft white bread) of the Value 6 in Cody. Friends of Anik's owned the motel and had given them a good rate.

"Not rotis again!" cried Priyanka.

At first Priyanka had seen the trip as a break from the motel. Normally, she spent most days hiding in one of the motel rooms watching cable TV and filling out Value 6 notepads with drawings and letters to friends back in India. But she soon realized the trip consisted of staying in other Value 6's across the state. Staying with other Indians whose only link with them was ownership in a motel chain.

"Sweetie, soon we will be back home to Uncle and Aunty's, and you can have all the rice and curries you want, but for now, rotis."

Priyanka stared out the window. Last night they had eaten rotis dipped in the last of a curry stored in an old jam jar.

Look, Kavita got sugar back at the McDonald's. Let me put some sugar on it for you." Madhu took thin discs of bread and put sugar on them. It wasn't real sugar and it looked as if each pancake were coated in a white mold.

"Vikram, breakfast." She placed a roti on a thin napkin. She glanced out the window before looking to her husband. He was asleep.

The car had been slowly going off the road. But in the hassle of breakfast and finding a bottle of water that had rolled under the seats, no one had noticed. Vikram snapped awake and jerked the steering wheel to the left.

In that moment, the moment between accident and before accident, before before and after, Madhu's mind flashed to the cinema. About going to the cinema. Her father would take them once a month. To the old Rialto Theatre. The only theatre in town with a soda fountain. She and her brothers and sister would order Tutti Fruitis. It was a concoction of iced and whipped cream, canned peaches, nuts, and mango sauce. Madhu would mix it all together into a mush. The sweetness of the fruit, the cream, it stayed thick in your stomach throughout the whole show. And they would get there in a two-wheeled cart. Carried by a tired horse with watery eyes.

The drivers always pushed the poor animals to reckless rates. And in the streets, anything would spook them, from rickshaws to motorcycles. The carts were like the flatbed of a truck and on the sides were painted all sorts of disconnected scenes. From Jesus to Gandhi, JFK to film stars. The horse wore bells around its neck and in the cart was a thin mattress. Madhu was small as a child and always seated next to the driver. The drivers would always try to weight the cart evenly to avoid the cart teeter-tottering.

"In the back, in the back," he would say to Madhu's father, who would arrange himself carefully as to not stain his white button-down shirts and grey pants, a Parker fountain pen in the shirt pocket. Madhu's brothers would hang their legs off the back of the cart.

There was the constant tip of the cart as people got on or off. The ringing of the little bells. And Madhu would look at the street below her dangling legs. Feeling the undulation of the cart. *Up down, up down.* There were no belts. No staying inside the cart. Limbs swung like pendulums from all sides. *Up down, up down.* And yet, there were no accidents for them. But now, here was the car. Flipping. Rotis on the ceiling. Limbs not like pendulums. Limbs all mixed together. Peaches, ice cream, nuts, mango sauce. Rotis, ketchup, sugar.

The car rolled and all Madhu saw was her sugar-coated hand and a slice of blue sky and prairie behind it.

Padma Subramanian was known to everyone as Paddy.

"Like rice!" she would say when she met someone new. Her last name she would mumble or leave out, the repetition and her stressing of the *subra* like *cobra* left most newly acquainted with expressions that made her frown. Her own daughter Ru as a child told people their last name was Superman. She was now a senior at a college on the East Coast, far far from her classmates she perceived as reliving high school at various schools across the state. Paddy carried around a wallet thick with pictures of her. Here is Ru skiing! Here is Ru with our congressman! (She had gone to Washington on a school trip.) Or here is Ru in a salwaar kameez (looking distinctly out of place) at our last anniversary party! Paddy and her husband Raj had been married almost twenty-five years.

The Subramanians had resided in Casper for almost all the years of their married life. Raj was in oil and gas. He lived out on the prairie most weeks, making guesses at whether or not oil was sopping up the rocks. And Paddy liked to say she was one of the first Indians here. East Indian that is. She would laugh and shake her hair out when people asked if she was American Indian. "Indian-American," she would reply. "I am what Columbus thought he saw when he came here." She was, in her mind, a one-woman Indian ambassador (like the car: strong, timeless). She spoke at schools and churches, and sometimes at civic groups in which she drank watery iced tea while regaling the audience with stories about India.

She met the Patels weeks after the accident. Madhu had been in a coma for three weeks and was finally coming out of it. Her first words were a jumble of English and Hindi (water, achaa, mirchi, jar, mujhe kamraa chaahiye). Paddy, who was from Chennai, had been on a list of possible translators for the hospital for years but had rarely been called in the years she had lived in Casper. Once, a Bengali woman who was caught shoplifting diapers from Kmart had been running out of the store, only to trip and break her arm. It was not the hospital that had called Paddy, but the police. The woman simply refused to speak. They weren't sure if she understood her Miranda rights, or even why she was being held. The police were disappointed that Paddy couldn't speak Indian. But she couldn't speak Bengali, so the woman's circumstances were never known.

The only other time she had been called to the hospital was for another car accident. An Indian woman had been in a wreck in rural Wyoming. She had been transported to the main hospital in Casper. She had spoken in a low voice to Paddy. She was fleeing California to get away from her husband who hit her, and she wasn't used to driving. She had bruises around her eyes that looked like smudged kohl. She was trying to get to friends in Wisconsin. Later Paddy watched as her husband came and got her. There was nothing she could do. She was just the translator. She only was supposed to relay that the woman wanted vegetarian broth and her tea sweet and milky.

With the Patels, it wasn't Madhu Paddy knew first. It was Vikram and the children. Sameer was the only one besides Madhu to suffer serious injuries. He had been in a coma for a few days and had some internal bleeding. When the paramedics first found him, they had thought he was bleeding from his stomach. But it was dozens of packets of ketchup that had exploded on impact that had stained his too big t-shirt. He had recovered well, and was now walking around. Vikram, Kavita, and Priyanka had relatively minor injuries considering no one was wearing a seat belt. In some ways, their old car had saved them. It was a Chevy Impala, which long ago had been left at Anik's motel. It was low to the ground and, due to its sheer size, had not flipped too far. It had been the car of an oil roughneck who came into Anik's motel once a week or so to shower and sleep in a proper bed. He had asked Anik to watch the car, as he needed to take care of some business. Four years had passed, and the roughneck had never been back. For a long time Anik had been suspicious of the car and left it sitting in the parking lot, the keys behind a Ganesh that stood near the front desk. But after two years, Anik began to move it around into different parking spaces, occasionally taking it for a drive by the missile base. Although when the winter came, he left it alone. Cleaning ice and snow off a car that wasn't his seemed beyond his capability. When Vikram and Madhu came to Cheyenne, the car became theirs. Anik owned a silver minivan with the name of the Value 6 stenciled onto the door and a small Honda that his wife Savita drove.

For Madhu the car was a thing of great space. In India, she rarely rode in cars. Occasionally, if there was a special task to be done, like when she bought her wedding sari or went on a visit with out-of-town guests, a white Ambassador would be hired. Madhu always felt sorry for the drivers who would sit in the hot car while they went in and did their business. As a teenager, she'd sometimes slip ten rupees to the driver so he could buy a cup of tea while she went into air-conditioned coolness. The Impala was beige and in poor condition, but it was theirs. In India, the most that she and Vikram had owned was a scooter. When Priyanka was little they'd prop her up on the handlebars as they moved through the streets, a scarf around both of their faces so as not to breathe the fumes. Otherwise, she had ridden in auto rickshaws, pressing her back into the seat to feel the safety of the thin plastic canvas-like top above her.

Paddy had known plenty of Indians who had passed in and out of her life since she lived in Wyoming. They all seem to move like covered wagons on a trail bound for somewhere else. And driving seemed to be one of the things they did worst. She always marveled that for doctors, engineers, and computer programmers, the mechanics of a car seemed to cause them so much trouble. She had concocted a series of stories to put the fear of driving in any new arrivals. She realized that other drivers, empty spaces, and semi trucks did not promote the level of caution that she hoped to evoke. So instead she told exaggerated stories of deer and elk that would run out into the road; not only would the car be wrecked, the animal would be hurt. When blank faces still looked back at her, she mentioned how cattle sometimes rambled into the road and that Wyoming is a "fence out" state. Ranchers didn't have to fence their cattle in; others had to keep them out. The thought of killing cows at high speeds seemed to do the trick. Karma was a better deterrent than any threat of death.

She spent countless hours taking new Indians shopping for Tupperware and car seats. Again, she lied when she felt it was necessary. She told new mothers that they could lose their visas if they were caught driving without a car seat, their children detained. They could be deported for speeding tickets.

But she didn't know the Patels before their accident. They had missed her talks on the dangers of caravanning, why speed was not their friend. There was no point in lecturing Vikram. Madhu was lying with her black hair knotted like a shadowy halo around her head. She was paralyzed from the neck down.

When Madhu first came to America, Vikram had already been working in Cheyenne for five months. She was not a new bride, unlike Anik's wife. She knew that the motel would be hard work. But she had three children, and for that reason she decided to be silent about her unhappiness at leaving India. Because in India she was essentially free. Her in-laws lived with Anik in Cheyenne. In India, she and Vikram had their own flat behind a sweet shop. Once a day, Madhu would wander next door trying to decide if she wanted ladoos or barfi with their afternoon tea. After school the children would have milk tea and sweets, telling her of their day in school, what they had seen on the walk home.

It was Vikram who wanted the move; he claimed the computer industry was better in the states. They were doing fine in India. But doing well in America — that was something completely different. Madhu sighed and thought how competitive Vikram was with Anik. Vikram claimed to miss his family. They decided to go to Wyoming. The first thing Madhu had noticed out of the plane window when she arrived were the roads. Long straight lines like a map below. *I am Magellan. I am Columbus. There is a map beneath me*, she had thought. The roads cut through the brown. They seemed to be pointing, urgently, insistently.

She read a book at the library called *Let's See the U.S.A.* There were pictures of Eisenhower and the first highways. Empty stretches of road with nothing but the bleary streak of a black roadster. No cows. No bicycles. No people in the way making you stop nearly every few yards. No children with their faces pressed into the glass pushing hands into a sliver of open window. She knew then she would learn to drive. Instead of a scarf being tied around her mouth to stop the choking smog, she would tie a scarf around her head. And looking that first day at the Impala, she saw her dream would come true.

Vikram had already been driving for a month by the time she arrived with the children. Anik met them at the airport in Denver. His minivan was the only thing that would hold all their luggage. Madhu's bags were loaded down with Chandrika soap and bitter melon chips; crisp saris wrapped in newspapers, their creases marked from good coal irons; hot mixture; and two boxes of ladoos wrapped in dhotis she had carried just for Vikram. Vikram was anxious the next day to drive them around Cheyenne. He wanted them to see the missile base (or the outskirts of it) and the stadium where Frontier Days was held. Vikram and Madhu laughed at the idea of going to a rodeo. Anik's motel was a small sponsor of Frontier Days. He figured if he was going to benefit from the tourists, he should give something back. The thought that cows were roped and wrangled did not seem to faze him.

"They don't eat them, no? If they killed the animals, I would object. But people are seeing how strong these fellows are…it's not bad."

Madhu thought Anik was a bigger fool than she remembered. In June, she signed up for driver's education through the local high school. The class was filled with bored fifteen-year-olds who were trying to spare themselves taking the class during the school year. Madhu studied her textbook every night. She learned all the signs that were foreign to her — the yellow diamond with the prancing stag, that *Ped Xing* was not a foreign language but a shortened version of "Pedestrian Crossing."

It was the films that she liked best. Mini lessons in the dangers of not being predictable. *Signal 30* was the most enjoyable. It was made in the 1950s. Madhu enjoyed the sights of soda shops and circle skirts as much as the footage of a car wrapped around a tree, the high school football star dead. Her next-favorite film was a cautionary tale of drinking and driving. This one was made in the 1970s, and it featured girls with bouncy hair, big corsages, and dresses with elastic tops that seemed to float under their shoulders. For these teens, their prom night was ruined by a few careless drinks. The carnations from Jodi, the heroine, were crushed under the wheels in which she also has her untimely death. Madhu spent weeks mastering the unexpected — scanning parked cars along the curb as you drive to make sure a door doesn't fly open, checking your blind spot, knowing where runaway truck ramps were. But when driving with Vikram, her lessons seemed to come to nothing. She became nervous and flustered. Vikram had begun smoking in America, and his smoke and fooling with the ashtray made Madhu swerve when behind the wheel. In Driver's Ed, she was the best student in her class. Days in which the class went to the practice track, she often spent an hour happily driving in circles, their teacher (the high school football coach) indifferent to Madhu's laps. His eyes moved toward the real laps of two young sophomores, who giggled at nearly everything he said.

And so Vikram took over the driving. He told Madhu he only wanted her to have a driver's license for an ID, even though she passed her driver's test on the first try.

"Now you have the license. You can write checks, rent movies. But you get Savita or me to drive you. The real roads are not like that course you go on."

"Vikram, I was top of my class. I even know how to drive a stick shift." Madhu had spent one day miserably having the car die every time she let out the clutch.

"No, Madhu. You have a license. You can use in it in an emergency. These roads…the pickup trucks, the weather. No driving." And so wherever they went Vikram sat squarely in the driver's seat.

The trip to Yellowstone had been Priyanka's idea. She wanted to see bears and a geyser, which she pronounced gee-zer. They had been working for months without a break, and Anik suggested that April, the off-season, was the time to go. They would stay with other Indians along the way, another Patel family in Cody, and the Singhs in Cooke City.

In fact, April was not the time to go. The east, west and south entrances to the Park were closed. Only the north entrance was open to wheeled vehicles. To traverse most of the park, you needed to be in a snowmobile or snowcoach;

the Impala was not made for hard winter driving. While in Cheyenne the snow was only in thin strips along the snow fences, packed against the rails in crystalline flakes, it was deep and drifting in the park. They had seen little wildlife, Vikram had vetoed eating out, the geysers had seemed like watery sputtering fireworks (only Priyanka, Vikram, and Sameer saw Old Faithful; Kavita and Madhu stayed with the car to save the cost of the snowcoach).

The Value 6's in both Cooke City and Cody had been replicas of Anik's place in Cheyenne. Except for the potted plants in the foyer and the various gods placed by the cash register, it was as if Madhu was vacationing in her own home. Vikram insisted that Madhu, Sameer, and Priyanka help clean rooms to show they weren't ungrateful. Sameer loved to fill the washers and pull sheets out of the dryers. The Singhs had Hispanic maids who let Sameer push their carts, smiling when he knocked towels onto the floor. Priyanka filled motel message pads with stories. Kavita stayed close to Madhu. She was the slowest in adjusting to Cheyenne. The wind and the open space made her cry. She often asked for sweets and refused to wear socks with shoes. She would begin kindergarten in the fall and still couldn't use Western toilets with a regular ease. In India, they had a squatter.

After the accident, Paddy saw Madhu every day. At first, Madhu rarely spoke to her.

"*Main Hindi nahin bol sakta hun.* I don't speak Hindi," said Paddy, wanting Madhu to tell her that her Hindi was not actually too bad.

"*Iskaa daam kyaa hai?* How much is this?" Madhu whispered back.

Vikram had to help run the motel and could only come up to Casper on weekends. The children were in school. And so it was left to Anik (who thought he understood American doctors better) and Vikram's parents to take turns staying in Casper. The Value 6 in Casper was not owned by Indians. The Indians in Casper tended not to own chains. Instead they owned motels in which they could decide on the name — The Royal Inn bumped up against I-25. The Camelot was across from the abandoned refinery. Paddy and Mr. and Mrs. Patel spent hours talking of Madhu's medical care. Vikram and Madhu had no health insurance. Accidents were not part of their American plan. Mr. and Mrs. Patel were more concerned that the hospital would think that they were Muslim. They brought a diorama/temple with Ganesh standing on a rat and set it up near Madhu's bed. It plugged in and lit up. When a button was pushed, a little song of prayer could be heard. The nurses delighted in turning it on. Madhu moaned from her bed. She didn't like the song and the odd hours in which it was played.

When the hospital realized that the Patels had no money, they transferred Madhu to a kind of waiting floor. A purgatory of beds for people they didn't quite know what to do with. She received care, in that they changed her sheets and catheter, but she had no rehabilitation. Her bed was a funny air bed, which rotated from side to side to keep her legs from atrophying. The children and Vikram came up most weekends to see her. But the room was mostly silent. There was nothing to say. Priyanka's broken nose angrily stood out from her face. Sameer enjoyed watching the bed rotate. Kavita wore socks under her sandals.

Paddy Subramanian called the governor's office and anyone who would listen to get Madhu on Medicaid, to get the state to help. She appealed to the churches she spoke at, to the Kiwanis, Rotarians, and Lions. A few donations trickled in. The Department of Health asked Vikram to fill out forms.

And as Madhu woke up more and more to her new life, Paddy tried to explain the world to her. Why they came in and took her blood pressure, how she must eat when the feeding tubes came out and where her excrement was going. And to the nurses, Paddy also translated. To an Indian woman, modesty was very important. Often the nurses on duty left Madhu's legs exposed, her gown half hanging open. Madhu could not change this. Paddy berated them if she found Madhu uncovered.

"No, no, keep covered! In our country, if a woman showed her leg like this, she'd be a ho," she said to a nurse with teddy bears dancing across her V-necked scrubs. Her daughter Ru had called her this on her last vacation home when she refused to let her and her boyfriend sleep in the same room.

Madhu told her that before the accident the only person to touch her naked had been Vikram, and even then, they touched in the dark. Paddy carted in her own idea of healing foods, curd rice and rasam, idlis and sambar, which mostly the Patels ate. Kohl liner and bindis were brought in and Paddy made up Madhu's eyes. Looking in the mirror Madhu was silent, yet smiled. Paddy painted her toenails and fingernails Vixen red. Her heels were cracked and rough, the soles of her feet calloused. Paddy knew they would grow soft in the coming months. Her fingers, which had been rubbed raw by bleach and laundry detergent, would become like sari silk, smooth and cool.

It was her hair that had Paddy most concerned. Madhu had multiple IVs coming out of her arms and neck. So her nurses and doctors in their constant rotations had tried not to get her hair tangled with the plastic lines. Madhu's hair had been long and silky, falling down to her knees. Now it was a matted nest above her head.

As it happened, Paddy lived next door to a beautician named Becky. She was a small, severe creature, whose experiments with hair color had left her own hair in a wiry state. She made up for her small stature by wearing tall, wedged shoes. She was often outside her house talking on her cell phone, a cigarette balancing in her lips. Becky was full of bad ideas, her latest being Saran-Wrapping an old dog kennel in hopes of creating a small greenhouse. Inside the plastic-wrapped chain link was an odd array of geraniums and beans, corn and basil. But Becky liked a challenge, and the thought of cutting a quadriplegic's hair was too good to pass up.

"I can cut any kind of hair," said Becky. "Once, when I was in beautician school down in Denver, we had to cut black hair. This little black kid comes in. Cute as a button, that kid. When I was done, his dad looked at him and told me I must have cut a lot of black hair in my life. I told him I'd never cut black hair before. But I grew up on a ranch and had sheared a lot of sheep. He didn't like that at all. Told my instructor I was racist." Becky looked to Paddy for confirmation that she indeed was not racist, but misunderstood.

"Well, Madhu's not black. Just paralyzed," she replied.

Becky packed her scissors and hairspray in a tackle box. Taking one look at Madhu, her hopes of donating the hair to some organization for bald children went out the window. Madhu's hair was not only knotted, it was dirty. Gravel and sugar still clung to the recesses of her part. Becky worked with the same kind of wild pruning Paddy had seen her do on the lilac bush that bordered their houses. Paddy had a vision of Madhu looking like a pixie when it was all over, her face framed with hair she never thought possible. Instead, Madhu looked a bit like the Bride of Frankenstein. Her short hair stood on end in a way that made her look shocked, rather than elfin. Becky tried to lacquer her hair down with gel.

"Without washing it, this is the best I can do. We could give you some highlights…" Becky smoothed Madhu's hair into a greasy pompadour.

Paddy interrupted. "I love it. I love it. It looks like Audrey Hepburn. Or like you've been on a pilgrimage. You can see your face now."

She said this while digging in her purse for eyeliner and lipstick in hopes that with makeup on, Madhu wouldn't notice how badly she had been shorn.

"Short hair is so easy to care for. You just wash and go." Paddy gripped her own bun like a control knob and sighed, then cringed when she realized Madhu wouldn't take care of her hair. She would never wash her own hair again. Becky already had lost interest; she fixed her own hair with its bleached forelock in the bathroom mirror.

All around Madhu was a curtain of lost hair. Her hair, which had been oiled so carefully with coconut oil and strung with flowers, hair that Vikram had let flow over him the first time they made love, hair that caused American women to stop and touch it, was gone. Coils of hair hung around her body, disconnected from her frame.

Paddy didn't know what Vikram thought of the haircut, but she did register his surprise at finding out that Madhu would never walk again. The doctors said that Madhu's spinal cord was bruised and swollen and, as the swelling went down, perhaps the nerves would work again. They couldn't say. Vikram seemed to only hear part of this. He was sure that the swelling would go down and that all her body needed to do was rewire itself to receive messages. Paddy, always translating, told him it wasn't quite that simple.

The costs of Madhu in the hospital began to mount. A group called Caring Hands came over and gave Paddy and Vikram estimates of her care. The estimated cost of the first year of treatment was almost $600,000. On the bright side, the cost each subsequent year would be around $100,000. The caring hands asked if the motel in Cheyenne was handicapped accessible.

Madhu had never spent much time wondering if she

loved Vikram. They had been married for thirteen years. She met him when she was twenty. Marriage had come into her life much like school. She was expected to do it. She liked Vikram, and her sister had laughed that it was a love match rather than a real arranged marriage. Madhu laughed as well but knew that if she had her choice, she would not marry at all. But it wasn't as if she had much of a career. She had studied mathematics in university because she liked the logic of it. She could sit down and just solve a problem. She laughed over her friends who spent long hours writing essays on Spenser and Hopkins. She could finish her work and be at the movies eating fried banana chips in time for the early shows.

Vikram was in most ways a good husband. He took her for picnics near a temple she once said she liked. He bought her tapes of Hindi film music. He loved the children and walked them to school each morning. His only fault was a prostitute he often saw and had been seeing for years. Madhu had discovered her by accident. Coming home from a shopping trip with a cousin, she saw them both, in a doorway, partially obscured behind the coiling iron grillwork, kissing. She was a strange dark woman with eyes rimmed in kohl. Afterwards Madhu began to see her everywhere, and the shop owner told her she was a prostitute. She wore jeans and T-shirts and kept hair very short, almost like a man's. Madhu would see her buying cigarettes and leaning against the shop counters, her gold chain skimming the glass countertops. Madhu only felt bad for her, for the fact she was a whore. She lived her life at someone else's beck and call. She had no life to call her own.

After that, Madhu relaxed. She no longer felt guilty when she pretended to be asleep when Vikram touched her. She told him one day over coffee and Mysore pak that she didn't want to have sex anymore. That he should get it from his whore.

It was coming to America that had changed how Madhu was touched. Vikram slowly began to touch her hair, squeeze her shoulder. And knowing that he didn't have anywhere to go, she began to sleep with him again. They would sometimes go to the honeymoon suite, a room Anik decorated all in red. From the carpet to the walls, everything was a shade of burgundy. It was a bit like being in a clot, a womb in which the world of the Value 6 didn't exist.

And so that was the first question Vikram asked the doctors. Could they have sex? Paddy sighed. The doctors looked uncomfortable.

The head doctor sighed as well. "There is no reason, Mr. Patel, that a person with a spinal cord injury cannot lead a very normal life. Sexual function, although different, is of course not out of the question. Your wife needs to get used to her catheter. She is gaining some movement in her right hand, and for that we are hopeful. But the trauma to her spine is significant, and she will always be paralyzed."

Paddy found out weeks later that Vikram had already bought a ticket for Madhu to go back to India. He explained to Paddy that there she could live with her own parents, be around her friends and family. He and the children would stay in Cheyenne.

She was furious with him. She explained that not only would Madhu be stigmatized in her village, but the concept of handicapped accessible was not one known in her family's home.

"She'll be left in bed all day, Vikram. And you heard the nurses. If the catheter bag isn't changed properly, she can get an infection. And since she can't feel down there, she could die. This is crazy. Take her to the motel. If she isn't around the children, she'll go mad. Your mother will help her."

But Vikram would not listen to her. The meekness he had displayed for weeks had worn thin. Even his parents, who had thanked Paddy at first with sweets and food, began to frown when she arrived. It was Madhu who looked to Paddy, who whispered between cracked lips that she didn't want to go back to India. There she would be a nothing.

Madhu was transferred to a nursing home in Cheyenne months after arriving in Casper. Paddy flew on the airplane that transferred her. Madhu had cried at the suggestion of riding in an ambulance. The open road scared her. Paddy took pictures of the journey, since it was something novel for her as well. Posed around Madhu was a throng of white nurses, each one smiling, and one posing with Ganesh. In the plane, you could see the mountains through the window behind Madhu's head. Drool came out of her mouth, her expression blank. Snow sat on the peaks like sugar.

Paddy didn't visit her much once she was moved to Cheyenne. She felt now that Vikram and the children could see her every day, Madhu didn't need her to brush her hair and make up her eyes, to speak to her in halting and broken Hindi.

The state Department of Health and Social Services called months later to ask if Paddy would speak as an advocate in a hearing on whether or not Madhu should remain in the U.S. She was not officially a ward of the state, but as the state had footed most of her medical bills (emergency funds had been released), they wanted some say in where her future lay; the social workers had called this convening. Paddy had campaigned hard to get her state support, had helped Vikram file forms, and now she was leaving? Vikram for his part bought the tickets for India. Savita told Paddy over the phone that he had a new bride coming out the following spring. His parents had arranged it.

At the hearing, Vikram lost his temper. He cried to the judge that Madhu could no longer be a good wife or mother. She could hardly move. Her rehabilitation had been very slow. That in India, she would be with her family that didn't work the hours he did. She could have all the comforts she grew up with. Paddy countered that Madhu was this way because of him. Because he been driving for hours without breaks, because the open road and car had beaten him. Paddy told the judge how Madhu would be treated in India, how she would miss her children.

In the end, Madhu was given a permanent room in the nursing home in Cheyenne. Paddy visited her and laughed that she was like a black sheep amidst the white hair of the nursing home. The staff wheeled her to the craft tables where she watched arthritic hands piece together puzzles and play canasta. Three times a week a van from the home took her to the motel and sat her in the room where they served continental breakfasts. She waited for the children as they filed in from school, each one of them filling bowls of cereal and drinking apple juice from the juice machines.

It was when her catheter bag began to be bloody that the nursing home called Paddy again. Could she come down and ask Madhu what was happening? It was all right if Madhu and Vikram wanted to have sexual relations, the staff just needed to know. They needed to clean her and be sure the catheter hadn't been moved.

It had been weeks since she had seen Madhu. She sat slumped in her wheelchair in a pair of sweatpants one size too big. Her fingernails still had the traces of Vixen Red she had painted on months before.

"Madhu, you have to tell these people if you are having love with Vikram. They must know. Don't be embarrassed. Are you making love?"

Madhu looked at Paddy and shook her head no.

"Madhu, we know you are. This is a matter of health; don't be silly. Are you having sex with Vikram?"

Again, she shook her head no.

Paddy's patience was wearing thin. She hadn't driven

two hours to hear denials.

"Do you have a friend in the nursing home?"

Madhu looked at her with a sort of surprise at her naiveté. "Sometimes it's Anik. Other times Papaji. Vikram only watches. He won't touch me. He does that to Priyanka instead."

The words took a minute for Paddy to translate. Her Hindi went through her head like a tape.

"Mr. Patel and Anik have sex with you? They rape you? Vikram and Priyanka?"

"They'll only stop if I agree to go back to India. But I cannot leave Priyanka. I don't feel it. It's like the accident. It goes fast, and I can believe it is not my body, this is not me. It's okay."

Paddy, of course, called the police, and they took Priyanka away from the Value 6. She had never liked Anik, but Mr. Patel had seemed mild mannered and kind. He wore a windbreaker and a tweed hat. He always got Paddy coffee when she was in the hospital. He had promised her that when Ru married, Savita would come to Casper to do her mehndi. When Madhu heard about the police, she recanted her story. She claimed Paddy was a bad translator, that Vikram would never hurt the girl. Priyanka came back. In counseling she had said nothing. The rape test was inconclusive.

For Madhu her life had not flashed before her eyes as the car flipped. Her life flashed before her now as she sat watching Bingo games and talk shows. The smell of jasmine in the morning; the first taste of tea of the day; the shot silk sari she got when she came of age; standing at Kanniyakumari where the Indian Ocean, the Bay of Bengal, and the Arabian Sea meet; the cowboy hat she bought when she first arrived; the postcard of a jackalope that hung on the mirror of their room in the motel. She knew a new woman would come. To feed the children and sleep with Vikram. *I am Magellan. I am*

Columbus. There is a map beneath me. Madhu would learn the geography of her body, its borders taking her into the recesses of home and heart.

Curating Your Life

In Chennai, paradise could be found on every road. The Jolly Paradise Bakery was on one street, on the next, Paradise Tailors. The New Paradise Hotel was squeezed between a juice shop and a beauty salon. Paradise Biryani was alongside a chicken shop, while two streets over was a Paradise Medicals.

And what to do with all this heaven? It came at you everywhere you walked. And yet.

And yet, I jumped at the bawl of an auto rickshaw's horn. I stumbled when grazed by a passing motor scooter. I leapt aside when long company-owned IT buses filled with workers going to call centers careened by. I stepped in shit on the roads and usually arrived at work with my shirt damp with sweat, my heart beating fast, as I made the ten-minute walk quickly, averting my eyes from the men who lined the street outside tea shops, drinking their morning coffees and laughing with each other. It seemed I could make hell out of paradise.

I lived with two other Americans in the bottom floor of a yellow house. We were less than two miles from the seashore, living below a Mrs. Prabha, a woman we rarely saw in the daylight. Instead, she would make her inquires of us through the bars and mosquito netting of our windows before dawn.

"Mark!" She would call to my roommate in a half whisper, half hiss. "You have received a package! I will leave it on the steps."

"Kate! Kate!" her voice louder with every repetition. "Kate, the plumber will be in today! Lock your things! I will leave padlocks on the front step."

Our house was in a constant state of erosion. The plumbing backed up. Our outlets would shock us when we tried to plug in toasters, radios. The inverter refused to work when the power cut out, which was often. And lastly, we had discovered, when the monsoons began, that our house flooded. As the rains came in, mold grew like velvet contusions on our cupboard doors, on clothes. The whole house felt moist and sodden. We ran our ceiling fans twenty-four hours a day in an effort to keep things dry. But as our boss explained to us, Mrs. Prabha was one of the few landlords who would not only rent to foreigners, but also rent to boys and girls who were not married.

Mrs. Prabha rarely called to me. And when she did, she used my Indian name, not Rae, which everyone else called me. "Raema! Raema!" Her intonation rising like a loaf of bread. "Raema! You are leaving your fans on when you are not home. Raema, don't do this!"

She only scolded me. To Mark and Kate it was "Are you settling?" To Kate, she offered cooking lessons, to take her shopping for the best salwaar kameezes, to take her to her astrologer (who had predicted a year ago she would be dead in five years). But on the few occasions when I would meet her at our large wrought-iron gate, she would look at me and tell me that she had a treadmill I could use. She told me I needed to get a facial. She didn't think I looked as pretty, as the walking in the sun to and from work was making me more dark and tan.

"Too dusky, Raema!" she scolded me.

The dampness that spread into our house, I felt inside of me. My very core since being in India felt gummy and thick. I lay in bed in the mornings and felt heavy-limbed and tired, even though since arriving I was getting, some nights, almost ten hours of sleep. In the evenings, before I climbed into bed, I would sit cross-legged on the floor on a thin bamboo mat that molded when wet. I would sit there and imagine the Wyoming sky. So blue. So clear. I pictured nothing but prairie filled with sagebrush, sego lilies, rabbitbrush, and endless open. I saw the Big Horns. The Absarokas. The Wind Rivers. The Snowies. I pictured mountain ranges like vertebrae, rising up after miles and miles of empty open range. I thought of dryness. Of how my nose bled in the winter from the altitude and lack of moisture. I slept most nights with a humidifier. I felt the air in India. While back home, I felt nothing—or perhaps the air felt so natural, you didn't have to think about it.

Mark and Kate were from San Francisco and Boston. They were twenty-three and semi-fresh out of college. Both of them had worked one office job since graduation. I tried to hide the fact that I was thirty. That I was probably too old for the internship we all had at the Pink Lotus Foundation. I'd thought in the few emails we had exchanged before arriving in India, that I would have the upper hand. That I was the Indian.

The roommates kept blogs. They were members of all sorts of social networking sites. And that is how we met our circle of friends. A strange mix of people whom, in other circumstances, probably none of us would hang out with. *Ferengis*. All of us. There was Kit, who was studying dance and had a body so lean and muscled, I wanted to touch her. Her blog had pictures of dances she attended, temples she had visited. There was Hep, who was quick to tell us he was Canadian. He even had a small Canadian flag sewn onto his messenger bag as if to tell India he was not one of us—he was a more sympathetic creature from a land of maple trees and peace. I never really understood what Hep did. He was working illegally and told us that every six months he left India for Nepal or Sri Lanka to renew his tourist visa. But when he was in Chennai, he seemed to work at some sort of computer job. His blog featured him widescreen in Nepal, a mountaineer's hat on his head, climbing rope wrapped around his arm like a lasso.

There was a group I called the Ivies. All strikingly beautiful. Sturdy, rosy-cheeked, and well put together. All had Ivy League educations. India hadn't rumpled them as badly as the rest of our ragtag group. Whenever we met for drinks or for concerts, their linen pants would look pressed, their feet clean. They worked at non-governmental organizations and, I imagined, would head back to places like New York or Chicago. Places where good jobs would open like a ripe clementine. For them, social change was a profession, a year in India fitted in between undergrad and graduate school. By time they were thirty, they would be living in houses with granite countertops and in-home theaters.

There was the tech crowd. These IT-ers made U.S. salaries in India and were always suggesting drinks at five-star hotels and impromptu trips to Pondicherry where wine was easy to get. They spent most weekends at resorts near Mahabalipuram, drinking beer on the beach, weedy-looking boys in tight pants fetching them whatever they fancied. Their boring cubicle life that would have been reduced to a comic strip in the United States not only allowed them to live like sahibs, but to act like ones as well. For them, going native was the few minutes they negotiated for auto rickshaws. Their glee in saving ten rupees was trumped only by the fact that they all headed back to flats with sweepers that came in every day to scrub their shit from their toilets.

Lastly, there were the in-transits, people who came and went, who were passing through India on treks or travels. Studying yoga, coming to stay in ashrams, or just to bask on the beaches of Goa or Kerala. The in-transits wore a uniform that was a combination of East meets West—loose salwaar pants coupled with graphic American T-shirts, sari slips with fleece, jeans with ill-fitting woven tops. For accessories, they favored things made of shells, beads, and silver. They wore leather sandals with soles as flat as chapatis. After a month, I barely talked to the in-transits at parties. What was the point? They would be gone. And for the most part, they didn't want to talk to me. They wanted to talk whitey with other whites. Because even though I was American, it was hard to say to a brown face that you hate Indian food, the streets stink, and that you think all auto rickshaw drivers are thieves.

It happened at work as well. The other employees, all Indian, seemed disappointed in me. I didn't speak Tamil. I didn't cook Indian food. The only novelty it seemed was my accent. It delighted them to hear such a bland, American voice out of someone who looked so Indian, yet was in American clothes. The disappointment deepened once I started wearing salwaar kameezes to the office. Not because I wanted to. But because they were cooler. The cling of my T-shirts and waistbands of my jeans all made me sweat.

But everything that Kate did at the office was considered particularly charming. She mispronounced most everyone's name in the office. The boy who made tea and did our mail was named Kamal. I had a cousin with the same name. So I called him the way we pronounced it at home—Come-*ll*. Kate would arrive in the morning and in her sing-song way call, "Come-*all*! Come-*all*!" It was like she was summoning everyone. She would look at him then add, "When you are out mailing things, do you mind picking me up . . ." And she would lay out a little grocery list. He ate it up. He had a picture of her on his camera phone and came back with Diet Cokes and chocolate—whatever her whim was for the day.

For Mark and Kate, their lives in India were made infinitely more interesting on their blogs. Both their blogs were started before they arrived, and as a reader, I can tell you their lives picked up in India. Their blogs, which before India had been a chronicle of beers drunk and concerts seen, began to take on something new. It was, for the purposes of their computer diaries, a more glittering world. A world in which the words evoked another era: *expats, housekeepers, tailors*, and their morning drinks came not from the local cappuccino shop, but from an exotic man who pulled tea like a ribbon between two stainless steel cups. It seemed to take hyperbole just to describe what they saw. "There are cows! But no burgers! People sleep on the road! The markets are as colorful as peacock's feathers! It's as hot as an Indian curry." All the phrases fell out onto the page as sad clichés. Even Kate's blog banner was a riot of hot pink and orange. I was waiting for the day when a picture of folded hands in namaste would be added to the photo of the elephant that already merrily skipped across the top of the webpage.

They curated their lives on their blogs. They picked and chose the choicest bits to tell their readers back home in Boston or San Francisco or wherever their friends were. Kate described walks on the beach, wearing jasmine in her hair, buying vegetables from a man with a cart outside our door. Mark wrote about his film experience (he was an extra in a Kollywood movie), of smoking bidis, of being at Mahabalipuram, or Mahabs (since you know, he was a local). But I knew better. I saw them in the moments between their dazzling tales of adventure. I saw that the fridge, which was once full of mango pickle and biryani, chapatis and curries, was now being overtaken with blander foods: crackers, cheese spread, expensive jars of spaghetti sauce, cans of beans, white bread. Their stomachs were cracking open. I suspected the damp grew in them as well. Yet, in their blogs were pictures of them mugging next to crispy dosas, making rabbit ears behind cows with painted horns.

I began commenting on their blogs after we had been in India almost two months. Kate had written a rather tragic tale of how hard it was to buy alcohol in Chennai. How she missed wine! She wondered if any of her readers were going to Pondicherry or Bangalore soon—and if so, would they bring her wine? How she hated Indian beer and she wished, no, would give *anything* to have a nice cold microbrew.

It was true that buying booze in Chennai was a bit of a rigmarole. We usually sent Mark to the local wine shop with a roll of rupees and a backpack. Drunken men often sprawled out in front of the shop, and it felt rather, well, unsavory. I had bought alcohol only once, on a day that was so hot that I had spent the day at work craving a cold beer. At the wine shop, I got flustered, as making transactions through a grille at a shop where you can see none of its wares unnerved me.

"Two Kingfishers," I mumbled softly. Then added thank you in Tamil.

The man looked me up and down. Then disappeared into the back of the shop. He came back with two beers and wiped them down with a cloth. He wouldn't make eye contact with me.

Why they call them wine shops is a mystery to me, as there is no wine to be found here. Only drunk Indian men spending their whole day's pay on booze. Although, I have to admit, the beer here is cheap!

Kate's blog went on and on. I clicked on the comment icon, and a white box appeared before me. Writing as anonymous, I typed one word:

Anything?

Later that day at work, Kate deconstructed the comment. "*Anything?* What does that mean? I bet my friend Josh wrote that. He's always making sexual jokes . . ." she said.

But I could tell it unnerved her a bit. I waited two days and then commented on a post Mark had made about train travel. He had made a weekend trip to Madurai, and broke Indian trains down to pure disorder.

They run late, people eat and burp and sleep and fart. Why do all Indians seem as if they are packing their lives when they go away? I spent the night squashed between jute bags filled with food and cheap suitcases. Thank god for my headphones!

And so it went. I clicked again to the comments, and typed quickly.

Get on board.

What I wrote was true. I wanted Mark to get on board. It was the same thing I chanted to myself night after night when I was cross-legged on the floor, nights I spent dreaming about the silence of the plains.

I was on board when I decided to move to India. My parents were not. My father shook his head when I held up the letter from the Pink Lotus Foundation.

"They do good work! They help children!" I said.

My father fingered the brown nonsealing envelope the letter had come in.

"Why would you go there? You've already been. You can go with your mother and me any time. Why go with strangers?"

"Because I want to go on my own. I need my own India. I want to see the real India."

My father was a doctor, the only nephrologist in

Wyoming. His training and money made sure I didn't have to see the real India.

Because to me, the India presented to me on family trips was not real. Both my parents were from Kerala. Our trips to India consisted of moving from one relative to another relative's house. We ate. We occasionally went to tourist spots. We shopped. My urge to know India on those trips was trumped by my urge to shop. I bought things to encapsulate my experience. My grad school friends had oohed and ahhed at my embroidered pillowcases, bronze statues of Ganesh, the soft cashmere shawls I threw on casually before going out. When I graduated with my Masters in History, I wore a silk sari to my graduation ceremony. My mother had to put it on me.

It was when reading a blog about the tsunami that I came to know about Pink Lotus. It was a group that worked with women and children. What they did was vague to me. I saw the photos of women in saris and children, dark, flashing smiles with teeth as white as chalk. It was a frieze before me. As was every picture in *National Geographic*. Every show on the Discovery Channel. I thought, I will go. I will go and help them. This was the real India.

I took the letter out of my father's hand. "I'm going."

Our office was actually fairly small and the Foundation was more of a temp agency. We found volunteer positions for people coming to India. These positions usually involved helping in schools across Tamil Nadu. We also supported women who were learning local tribal crafts. Additionally, they let *ferengis* do things like sponsor a bicycle so a poor child could get to school. In theory, this was great. But in practice, our boss spent most of his time trying to untangle bureaucracy. As native English speakers, Mark and I spent the hours of our day writing grants, appealing for donations, writing testimonials and press releases. Kate had studied graphic design so she sat in front of the computer making posters, brochures—whatever would spread the good word of Pink Lotus.

However, it was Shreya who spent her time dealing with the volunteers.

Shreya Visweswaran was in her late twenties and had worked for Pink Lotus for almost three years. She was smart. And pretty. And had a wicked sense of humor. She dressed in long tunics and jeans, had short perfectly cut hair, and single-handedly kept the office running. She listened to the list of complaints from volunteers, smiled, and then got on the phone to fix it. Her cell phone seemed permanently fastened to her ear.

Shreya carried a stainless-steel tiffin container to work every day and at lunch time ate with a poise I had never seen before. She smiled in a mysterious way whenever Mark or Kate said anything, and I got the feeling she found them as ridiculous as I did.

At home one night, as I sat watching a pirated DVD of a romantic comedy on my laptop, my phone beeped. I ignored it. Spam flooded my message inbox. Offers to win kilos of gold or asking me to test my "love-meter" caused my phone to beep several times a day.

It was after I brushed my teeth that I picked up my phone and clicked on the message. It was from Shreya, and it was one line:

How are you?

No one had asked me this since being in India. Not even my parents. I didn't give them the chance. No, I preempted them with a PR version of my life. I told them the upbeat, the mundane. I didn't want to let them down. To tell them I didn't like the place that had formed and shaped them. My emails and phone calls were one long list of all the things I loved about India. I hardly gave them a chance to speak.

I wrote back one word: *Okay*. It was nearly midnight, and I wasn't sure if this was bad form, texting so late at night.

She didn't write back, but the next day at work, she asked if I wanted to walk with her to the shops. She was going to buy chocolate. As we walked, I spilled out how awful I found Kate and Mark, how crass they were. I told her about their group of friends. And then I told her the lamest thing possible. I told her I was in India to find my roots. As if I were a plant.

"You're different," she told me. "You'll understand India in a way they never can. Block them out." And it was as if Shreya gave me permission to comment. I then understood why everyone stood around talking white when we went out. It felt good to finally talk brown with brown.

I started commenting on their blogs several times a week. When Kate wrote about buying a sari and how hard it was to pick a color, I wrote, "*Eeny, meeny, miny, moe.*" When Mark told us about the temples of Kanchipuram and how it was not worth traveling there, I wrote, "*This land is your land. This land is my land.*" All references I believed to be obscure and baffling.

To my disappointment, sometimes they didn't even look at the comments. But other times they agonized over them. Kate noticed the times in which the comments were made and came to the conclusion they were being left by someone in India. All her friends would be asleep and not posting on her blog at 3 a.m. They never seemed to suspect me, but Shreya moved to the top of their list.

Mark was sweet on Shreya. They shared an office in the back, and he mooned around after her most days. Mark looked like an all-American boy—lean, tan, brown, floppy hair—but Shreya seemed immune to his flirtations. When

Kate wasn't flirting with Kamal, she tried to get Shreya in her good graces. She bought apples from the market and cut them up for our coffee break, she even made her a mix CD. Kate wanted Shreya's approval.

In her own social group, Kate already had it. Awhile back, she had over a group of Ivies. She made flavorless dhal and undercooked rice. She was telling them the story of a man in Delhi who had bought an old Airbus from Indian Airlines. The man had set it up in his land and was charging people for the experience of sitting on a plane.

"Now, mind you, the plane only has one wing! There're no lights or toilets, and people pay to just sit. I think his wife serves drinks. Can you imagine? People even buckle their seatbelts and watch a safety demonstration. The plane never takes off! I mean really. Only in India!" Kate laughed and the group of Ivies, who were gathered like gopis around her, laughed as well.

"Poor people travel to make money, rich people travel to spend it," said one of the Ivies.

Kate thought about this. "But in India, poor people spend money to travel to nowhere." She laughed and began to roll a joint.

It just so happened that Diwali fell the day after Halloween. I felt indifferent to both holidays. In my house, neither was celebrated much. My mother, with few other Indians to celebrate Diwali with, usually made nice food and lit a candle. For Halloween, she sullenly doled out chocolates.

On Halloween morning, Kate sat on the edge of my desk. Her brown hair was pulled back in a ball-like bun on the top of her head. Her glasses were fingerprinted. She put a small bar of Dairy Milk on my computer keyboard.

"Happy Halloween," she said.

I held the bar of chocolate. It was already melting.

"We're going to Clark's tonight for Halloween. There's an all-you-can-eat buffet and they're having a haunted house. I think the whole thing is about five hundred rupees. Do you want to come with us?" she said.

I think she was used to me saying no to any invites. But she still asked me to do things out of politeness. But I was interested to check out Clark's. I had ridden past it many times. You couldn't miss its signboard. CLARK'S: ALL-AMERICAN DINER! NACHOS! BURGERS! BBQ! PIZZA! IN HERE IT'S ALWAYS NORTH AMERICAN TIME! We had been in India over three months and truth be told, I wanted a burger. You could take the girl out of Wyoming, but not the Wyoming out of the girl.

"Yeah. I'll go. What time are you leaving?"

"Oh, really? We're meeting Kit and Hep at the water tank at six, and we'll all get autos from there."

"Are you dressing up?" I said.

"Yeah. Mark and I both. Wait to till you see what we are!"

Kate went back to her computer, and I saw the familiar chat box pop up in the corner of her screen. I was sure she was telling Mark I was coming. And I wondered what went uncurated about me when it was just them alone.

I took out my phone and texted Shreya.

Ferengis + Halloween = Fun.

A moment later my phone beeped.

Boum boum was her answer.

In Chennai, everything had been reinvented. Chennai was once called Madras. Mount Road was now a non-British version—Anna Salai. The addresses on every house bore two numbers, the old and the new. We lived at 45 Old/ 12 New 8th Cross Street. Instead of erasing the past, it was as if the future sat upon the past. Everyone said two addresses, gave two street names. Even when I told people I was going to live in

India, they would look at me blankly when I said I was going to live in Chennai. I would always add, you know, Madras.

As there were two of everything, those twins, past and present, rubbed up against each other and left everyone with a feeling of not knowing which was the real, what was the authentic. To me, India curated itself as well, as if to tell us that these things might have happened but they were gone. And what was left was a version that was so much better—it was Incredible India!

We often all walked home together. I sometimes stayed and pretended I needed to send email or do some work. But more often than not, Kate, Mark, and I ended up walking back at the same time.

All the shopkeepers knew Kate and Mark, and they would call out to them as they passed. Sometimes Mark would even have a cigarette with the men outside the juice shop around the corner.

As Mark stopped to smoke, Kate and I would finish the last bit of the walk ourselves. Often we walked in silence.

But tonight, the minute Mark separated from us, Kate told me she had something to tell me, but I had to swear not to tell, as Mark had sworn her to secrecy.

"Okay," I said.

"It's Shreya. She has a blog. And she is talking all kinds of shit about us," Kate's eyes were wide. We passed a fire-cracker stand.

I stopped. "What do you mean?"

"She has a blog. Like us. She doesn't use our real names—she calls Pink Lotus the Lily Pad. But she hates us and the office . . . you've got to read it."

"How do you know?" I asked.

"Mark. He had to use her computer the other day. And the address was in the drop-down box—the history. So he read it. Then sent me the link."

"What does it say?"

"What morons we are. She calls me Princess America. Mark's Captain White, and you're Princess Desi. Everyone has a nickname. What a bitch. I'm sure she's the one leaving comments on our blogs." She began to walk again.

I ran to catch up. "What does it say about me?"

"You know, that here you are trying to find your roots, what a cliché you are... you should read it. It's called *Ramblings of S*, on Blogworld. I'll give you the link tomorrow. Shit, is it almost 5:15? I have to get my costume." Kate's pace quickened.

I stopped again. "Oh. Hey, I just remembered, I forgot something at work. I left my camera on my desk. I need it for tonight. I want to take pictures. Halloween in India!" My voice sounded shrill.

I left Kate, and walked a block to the nearest internet place. I got on a search engine and clicked on the Blogworld website. I typed Ramblings of S and hit submit.

Seconds later, a pale pink screen flashed up. Her blog banner was spare, with only her blog name on it. Next to her profile box was a small photo of Shreya. She was partly obscured by a shadow, but I recognized the shirt she was wearing. I started to read her current post, but then clicked into the archives, starting with the entries from the month we arrived in India.

Princess Desi wears salwaars to the office, but thankfully no jasmine in her hair. I couldn't take not only a princess, but a fragrant one!

I reached up and touched my hair. In the past month, I had begun to wear jasmine. Fresh flowers were hard to come by in Wyoming, and buying a rope of jasmine every day made me strangely happy.

Princess Desi ate with her fingers at lunch today. Princess

America and Captain White did not. Princess Desi likes to pretend she is sophisticated and not from the jungli state that she is. But it was fun watching her trying to figure out how to serve herself more food with one hand.

Jesus. I may have been from Wyoming, but I had been eating with my fingers since I was a little girl.

Today took the cake, dear readers! Princess Desi asked me how to use the sprayer and hose after she went to the bathroom. Says she would like to stop using toilet paper. It was very hard for S to not smack her while giving her an answer. She prides herself on going native. It must be very hard slumming it on our level.

I read on. But then I looked at my watch and saw it was nearly six. I quickly paid for my time and ran to the water tank. Hep and Kit were already there. Hep was dressed as a mountaineer. He was wearing nearly the same outfit he wore on his blog. Kit wore a scarf on her head, a sari slip, a loose cotton top, and beads. She shrugged, "I'm a gypsy. What are you?" I touched my hair, I looked at the orange salwaars kameez I was wearing.

"I'm nothing." I paused. "I'm Indian."

Kit and Hep didn't answer as they began to laugh. Kate and Mark were approaching. Mark wore a long black wig and pink rayon sari. Kate had a plaid lungi wrapped around her waist and a tank top. Her dark hair was slicked with coconut oil. She swaggered in an odd way.

"We cross-dressed! We're Indians!" She sang out.

All around us on the street, people gawked. Did they have on self-tanner?

"I'm a hijra," said Mark. "Mrs. Prabha helped, but I think she was confused," he said.

"And I'm an Indian man." Kate had stuffed something

under her tank top so her belly protruded like a tumor. She took Mark's arm, "Come on, my date!"

I stood still. I didn't know whether to go with them or not. Kate loudly negotiated with two auto rickshaw drivers. And when push came to shove, I got in.

When we arrived at Clark's, all I could think was that I had been there before. But I hadn't. It was 1950s America replicated into the middle of India. The floor was a black-and-white chessboard pattern. The booths were a tomato-red vinyl. All over the walls were old advertisements for products like Burma Shave and Coke. We had a diner just like it in Casper. My mom and I often went there for milkshakes. On top of all this Americana were cobwebs; witches' hats laid out like cornucopias on the tables; on the buffet, a strobe light pulsed. The employees of Clark's, all Indian, were in costume. There was Raggedy Andy, a pirate, a ghost, a ghoul. I began to feel a little dizzy. The owner, a fat American man, wore a baseball uniform.

We had barely settled into a booth when Kate and Mark immediately began to mingle. Hep and Kit also left the table. On the buffet was an array of hot dogs, Chinese food, French fries, nachos—a strange hodgepodge of food.

But instead of the food, I thought about Shreya's blog.

She's just another ABCD coming to India to find herself.

She thinks a year in India will help her know herself. Princess Desi will never know herself. She's too busy distancing herself from Princess America and Captain White to know which end is up. Her angst about being Indian and her attempts to be a real Indian are just sad. She's a character out of a novel. She is Adela Quested, scared and frightened and never understanding what she is seeing, what she is. Which is an outsider. It's worse than the other two, because she thinks because her skin is brown and her parents grew up having coconut oil rubbed into their heads that she is somehow more.

I felt the tears coming to my eyes. Sitting in Clark's with Mark dancing in a sari and Kate and her gopis huddled by the buffet table.

Yesterday, I had commented on Mark's blog. He was writing about cricket. When we walked home at night there was usually a group of kids playing cricket in the street. When they saw us approach, they would always stop their game and watch us walk by. Mark compared the boys to how he and his brothers would play soccer in the street in their suburb of San Francisco. When a car came, they'd stop their game and wait for it to pass. Mark had a picture of some of the boys on his post. They had posed shyly. None of them was smiling, and one boy held his bat like a sash across his thin chest.

There was nothing about the post that was offensive. But I had typed in all capital letters one word.

ASSHOLE

I didn't realize I truly thought he was an asshole til I wrote it. But the truth was, I thought both of them were assholes. Assholes for getting India more than I did. Because they weren't afraid to do so many things. I hated them because they absorbed India in a way I could not. They rode bicycles without fear. They bargained with auto drivers, and if they found the price outrageous, would simply walk away. Kate bought an Indian cookbook and night after night, tried to cook. I thought that would be me. But instead, I sneaked out to the Video Point every night and rented pirated American movies. I spent nights huddled in my room, watching movies on my laptop, eating potato chips from Nilgiris supermarket. I rose up from the table. Kate and the gopis sipped Cokes from bottles. I took Kate's arm.

"I have to go. I'm not feeling well."

She frowned. "Do you want me to come with you?"

"No, I'll just get an auto."

I walked to the door, passing the entrance to the haunted house. Strips of crepe paper blew out and touched my arm. A white American family waited to enter. They were all blonde. One child was dressed as a ladybug, the other as a pirate. He had the same hat as one of the waiters. A sign outside the entrance read *Welcome to Hell*.

The dark mouth of the haunted house was black and open.

Boum Boum.

I turned around and went back to Kate. I took her arm again.

"It was me," I said.

"You? Where?"

"It was me. On the blog. Commenting. I don't know why . . ."

She was silent.

"I misunderstood. It was all a misunderstanding. I didn't mean to say the things I did. It was stupid. I take it back."

"Rae," she started to say something more, but I turned around and headed out of Clark's. Past the pirates, the dolls, the monsters, and other Americans.

Outside on the street, smoke filled the air. There was a large bang. And then a series of bangs. Diwali festivities were beginning to erupt.

I flagged an auto and mumbled the address. I didn't even begin to bargain.

As we pulled into Eighth Cross Street, the auto driver turned around and asked for the house number again.

"Forty-five Old. Twelve New." Or was it the other way around—Twelve Old, Forty-five New? "It's a yellow house." Which was it—the old or the new? The past or the present?

He stopped at our gate, and I could see Mrs. Prabha

upstairs looking down at me. Firecrackers popped and flamed out.

"Raema!" she called down to me. "Raema! You should not be taking autos at night alone. It is very dangerous!"

I could see her silhouette against the bars. I couldn't do anything right. My phone beeped in my pocket, and I pulled it out.

Is it horrible? ;-)

Shreya's text glowed on the screen.

"It's my parents," I called up to Mrs. Prabha. I opened the door of the house and sat on our charpoy.

I started to write her back. I wanted to sign it Princess Desi, to say a million things, but I felt grateful she was texting me even though I was so pathetic.

No. My fingers moved slowly over my phone. *Am on Cloud 9. Hot dogs.*

I pressed send and began to cry.

I sat in the dark for hours. Until I heard Mark and Kate's loud voices in the kitchen. I hadn't known the power was out, and I could hear Mark trying to get the inverter to kick in.

"Rae! Rae! I know you're here. Come here." Kate called out in the dark.

I moved out of my room quickly. The smell of the coconut oil in her hair filled the house. She was in the kitchen. I knew she was looking for the matches we kept near the stove. I silently opened the front door and ran out into the night.

The whole street was dark, save for a few houses with generators, which I could hear kicking in. Outside little diyas burned. The sound of firecrackers punched the air.

I headed for the main road. I looked for an auto to just go anywhere. Anywhere away from here. But only scooters and a lone cyclist moved before me. I started to walk. Up ahead, I saw an IT bus parked by the side of the road. The man whom I presumed to be the driver stood talking with an auto driver, a glass cup of tea in hand. I walked to the boarding side of the bus and leaned onto it to catch my breath. Along the side, scrolled below the windows was the phrase, "This is IT."

This was it. The door was open. I stepped up onto the bus.

I haven't seen the real India.

It was empty and I took a seat in the back. Higher up, I could see the street from a perspective that made me feel safe.

I've seen all the wrong things.

As I sat, the bus began to fill with a few scraggly call center workers. Women in salwaars and men in Oxford shirts and pleated pants. Nametags hung like collars around their necks. The driver climbed in, scarcely looking at who was on board. The engine sparked and we began to move.

Boum Boum.

No matter what sound you made, the echo was the same. The sound just came back louder and more amplified. You just couldn't say things and not have it return to you. It always came back. Wasn't that the lesson? You couldn't just change a name, rewrite history. The bus moved past shops illuminated by candles, past people waiting for other buses, past juice stands, and women selling jasmine stranded and coiled like pinch pots.

The real was not here. It was there. I was the person on the plane, pretending. Poor people travel to make money. Rich people travel to spend it. And the rest of us? We travel to reinvent, to change. I wanted something to happen. To leave my life in Wyoming and to see a glimpse of something else. And I wanted that something else to be nothing less than transformative.

For the passengers on the way to call centers, they were connecting to a new world. A world I knew, but could not name. It was, for them, a kind of paradise. For me, *not yet*. For them, *IT* was there. For me, not quite here.

Acknowledgements

To my agent Katherine Fausset — you are a reader of the best kind. I cannot thank you enough for loving stories, and for being the finest in every sense of the word.

I feel so fortunate to have landed at FiveChapters. Thank you to my editor, Dave Daley. He is the best advocate for the short story I know.

Many thanks to my mentors at the University of Houston and my teachers along the way — Chitra Banerjee Divakaruni, Rubén Martinez, Nick Flynn, Lanford Wilson, and Matthea Harvey.

The University of Wyoming English Department started me on my writing path and provided support to me at many stages of writing this book. Special thanks to Peter Parolin.

I was also blessed with the guidance of Marion Barthelme, John D'Agata, Alyson Hagy, Luis and Cindy Urrea, and Kevin McIlvoy. Thanks also to the places where my stories first appeared and all the editors that published them.

I am grateful to the Vermont Studio Center for its generous

assistance. Big cheers to the Sewanee Writers' Conference and Kevin Wilson in particular for their support. Thank you to the Sunday Salon Reading Series. Much appreciation to the Wyoming Arts Council, Artcore and Carolyn Deuel, and the Equality State Book Festival.

To the most magical place on earth: heartfelt thanks and love to the Bread Loaf Writers' Conference for giving me a community and inspiration. Special thanks to Noreen Cargill for her care, and big love to the whole back office crew.

Encouragement and love has been unwavering from Jill Meyers, Sasha West, Mónica Parle, Tiphanie Yanique, Emily Pérez, Tamara Linse, Cathryn Meyer, Laura Stevens, LuLing Osofsky, Holly Masturzo, Karen Eustis, Merrill Feitell, Justin Quarry, Eleanor Henderson, Ben Percy, Brad Watson, Kyle Hunsicker, Katherine Kline, Elena Touroni, Russ Weller, Dan Cepeda, Laura van den Berg, and Ted Thompson.

Thanks to the many people from Wyoming who are my family: Anne and Mike Watson, Teresa and Jacek Bogucki, David Tiistola, Bill Young, Greg and Gayle Irwin, and the whole community of Casper, Wyoming. And to Wind City Books for providing me with such a great bookstore.

Love to everyone I worked with at Tara Books in Chennai, India: Gita Wolf, V. Geetha, Jennifer Abel, C. Arumugam, and Sirish Rao.

My writing owes a tremendous debt to the unstoppable duo that is Antonya Nelson and Robert Boswell. To you both, I say thank you.

My family has been a rock: Skipper and Christine McConigley, Jim and Mary Lou Duffy, Vijaya Winters, Rajkumar Swamidoss, Stella Pandian, and Edith and Rana Thompson. My cousins have been the biggest cheerleaders—thank you.

To my grandmother, Irene McConigley, this book is because of you.

To Lila, Paul, Finn, and Aoife Martin: thank you for carrying you.

And most of all, to my parents, Nimi and Patrick—my compass is always pointed towards you. Always.